IN THE SPACE OF AN ATOM

Bruce M. Perrin

Cover Art by Courtney M. Perrin

Visit the Author at

BruceMPerrin.blogspot.com

Mind Sleuth Publications

ISBN-13: 978-0692836040 (Paperback)

TITLES BY BRUCE M. PERRIN

THE MIND SLEUTH SERIES

Of Half a Mind

Mind in the Clouds

Mind in Chains

STANDALONE NOVELS

In the Space of an Atom

Killer in the Retroscape: A Near Future Mystery

For all the latest on new releases, promotions, and book reviews,
subscribe to my blog: BruceMPerrin.blogspot.com

For My Family

Contents

What we usually consider as impossible are simply
engineering problems...
there's no law of physics preventing them.

MICHIO KAKU

AMERICAN THEORETICAL PHYSICIST, FUTURIST

1. Cornered ... not

The crack of the pistol shattered the silence of the musty storeroom as I dove to my left on instinct more than thought. The bullet slammed into a support column, dislodging a chunk of concrete that struck my forehead. Blood from the cut was already flowing toward my eyes as I sprinted down a darkened aisle between two sets of shelves along the outer wall.

"What the hell, Thomas," I yelled in confusion, wiping the blood away and continuing my rapid retreat. My vision had not fully adjusted to the dark at the back of the room, and I crashed into something laying in the aisle, falling to the floor on my knees. I grimaced with the pain, swearing under my breath so as not to give my new foe the satisfaction of knowing I was hurt. But it seemed he already knew.

"Easy there, Jeremy ol' boy," Thomas Jones called to me, pronouncing my name in the sing-song fashion someone might use with a toddler. "You don't want to kill yourself. No, let me do that." His calm, mocking tone was unnerving.

"Is this about the money? No one kills for a lousy $1,000," I yelled.

"You have no idea," Jones replied. He was correct; I had no notion why he wanted me dead.

I pulled myself over to the shelves to stand, but as I got up, my arms and legs started trembling. It was, I knew, the adrenaline pumped into my bloodstream as part of a fight or flight response. The problem was, it was just wasted hormones. There was no place to run and no way for me to fight someone armed with a gun. I needed calm. I needed to think, but my racing heart and sweaty palms were not making that easy.

"Let me shed a little light on your predicament," Jones said, and a bank of lights about 25 feet over my head came to life. When we had entered the storeroom, it had felt empty. The pool of light on that end had revealed little except open space and the ends of three sets of shelves. But now that the entire area was illuminated, I could see a space of perhaps 75 by 75 feet.

One side of the room was crammed with worn-out furniture—desks, tables, bookcases, chairs—all layered in years of dust. On the other side, shelves spanned the entire length and reached at least 15 feet into the air. They were filled with old computers, keyboards, displays, and terminals. There might have even been a card punch machine in there, as ancient as some of this equipment seemed. In my blind flight down the darkened aisle, I had tripped over a broken desk lamp that had been left there. Dust motes still swirled in the stale air at the site of the collision.

I was hoping that I could reason with Jones. I swallowed the lump in my throat, trying to master any tremble in my voice as I called out, "Seriously, Thomas, you can have the money. I won't say anything."

"I know I can, and no you won't," he answered, just loud enough for the sound of his voice to carry across the room.

So much for reasoning with him.

I came to the end of the aisle and wedged myself into a narrow gap formed by the end of a set of shelves and the far wall. But no sooner had I taken up my hiding spot than I realized how ridiculous it was to think it might conceal me. Jones would simply walk to the end of the row, spot me cowering there, and it would all be over.

As I extracted myself, my fear and disbelief morphed to determination. I clenched my fists so tightly that my nails bit into my palms. At a minimum, I had to make him work for his kill, make him hunt for me, make him hit a moving target. Maybe I could even inflict some damage along the way. Hoping to create some misdirection to mask my location, I grabbed one of those lights that clamp to the edge of a desk and tossed it over into the pile of furniture on the other side of the room.

Jones started laughing. "Nice try, Jeremy, but what ... you think I'm blind? Or was I supposed to shoot the lamp out of the air, like a clay pigeon?"

So much for misdirection.

The sound of Jones's footsteps told me he was slowly working his way down the aisle between the second and third sets of shelves, while I was still 'hiding' at the end of the first set. My eyes darted around the room, seeking a possible way out. When I stood on my tiptoes, I could just make out an exit sign, most likely above a door on the other side of the storeroom beyond the furniture. But if Jones had spotted a lamp flying in that direction, what chance would a running man have? And besides, the door would be locked. Who left an outside door to a storage area open? And yet, it was the only option I could see.

The aisles between the shelves were only about four or five feet wide, so in a break for the exit, my exposure would only be a second or two before I disappeared behind the pile of desks and tables. But was that too long? I gritted my teeth and feigned a dash across the aisle—a quick step out and a lunge back. No shot. No word. Hadn't he seen me or was he just baiting me?

"You pass out from fright, Jeremy ol' boy? Or just pee your pants and too embarrassed to come out? Hey, we're all friends here. I won't tell anyone. Yeah, you can be sure. I won't tell a soul about anything that happens here tonight."

What is with the ol' boy stuff?

In the five weeks I had known Jones, he had never addressed me that way. In fact, he rarely said a word to me, other than to grunt in response to my 'good morning,' often failing to even look up from his newspaper. He did so little around the lab that I had come to believe his job was to clean up after hours. And was that what he was doing now? Was he cleaning up some unfinished business for Dr. Johannes Schmidt, the man who had hired me and who conducted this research? But that seemed unlikely; Schmidt had left hours ago. He probably knew nothing of this.

"You know, I gotta lesson for you, Jeremy. Before you shoot somebody with a throw-away, you really should pop off a few rounds. I mean, take this one. It drags a bit more than I'm used to. But I think I got it down now. Shall we give it a dance?"

If he was trying to unnerve me and get me to do something stupid, I was winning the first battle. The continual taunting was serving to strengthen my resolve. What I was less certain about, however, was whether my life-or-death dash to the exit door was the stupid part he was trying to goad me into or not. It was a ploy that was dicey, at best. I took a deep breath and slowly released it, steeling myself for the sprint across the open area.

Or maybe I could ....

It had been a long time since I had played hide-and-seek as a kid, but I still recalled a strategy that had worked surprisingly well. It was, simply, 'go high.' I was always amazed that climbing up a tree 10 or 12 feet seemed to make me almost invisible. I remembered sitting there in the branches while my cousins trampled down every bush and shrub, overturned every table and chair, and scrutinized every corner and crevice in our hiding area.

Go high now meant on top of the shelves. Perhaps it would provide the cover I needed to get by Jones and back to the door we had entered. I was pretty sure he had not bothered to re-lock it, believing there was no way I could get past him. Unlike running to an exit that was probably secured and exposing myself in the process, I saw a glimmer of hope in this new stratagem.

The shelves were wooden units, built at a time when lumber was solid and construction was designed to last a lifetime. I had no doubt they would hold my six-foot-one-inch, 185-pound frame. All I had to do was climb to the top of the first set and slowly make my way back to the wall where we had come in. Fortunately, the top shelf on this outer unit was lightly used. The gaps between the antique equipment were wide enough for me to squeeze through. And maybe I could find a hundred-pound computer terminal to drop on Jones's head as I went by. I allowed myself a smile at the thought ... however unlikely it might be.

I started climbing up the outside of the first set of shelves, hand over hand, foot over foot. Just as I was reaching the top, however, my foot slipped off the board and drove into the outside wall, jarring my hands free. Falling backward, I grabbed the outer edge of the top shelf, stopping my 15-foot plummet to the floor below.

Even as solidly built as these shelves were, they were not that stable. They started to tip. Pulling myself up against the board to stop my backward momentum just seemed to accelerate the process. I managed to get my head out of the way just as the shelf I was on smashed into the second set. In turn, the second unit crashed into the third.

The room reverberated from the sound of the chain reaction, as a cloud of dust smelling of mold and burned-out electronics rose into the air. Fortunately for me, the first set of shelves came to rest on top of the second, sparing me from being trapped between it and the floor.

Jones, however, was not as lucky. The third unit slid away from the second as they collided, allowing both to fall to the ground. Just as they struck the floor, a shot rang out. Had it been aimed at me or merely the result of Jones's hand being jarred? But whatever it was, Jones had missed and he was now pinned against the floor, at least temporarily. This was my chance.

I wiggled out of the gap between the shelf and the ground, my heart racing, the sounds of the collisions still ringing in my ears. I ran to the door we had entered. Relief flooded through me as the door handle turned and I slipped back into the familiar confines of the equipment room.

This room housed the most incredible array of machines with racks filled with computers, power supplies, and displays, all humming and aglow when in operation. A reception room lay beyond, which was littered with posters and promotional materials that sang the praises of the company doing the research here. But the focus of everything in these two rooms was the object covering the passageway between them. It was the "Environmental Barrier" and it had changed as the study proceeded.

Initially, the Barrier had been made of tissue paper. Now, it was a one-inch thick piece of solid steel—one of those plates that road crews put over holes or new concrete on the highway. Over a week ago, I had watched as it had been carefully lowered into place with a thud.

What made the Environmental Barrier the center of all this hoopla was the fact that it was, mind-blowingly enough, penetrable. How the technology made that possible was well beyond me. I hadn't even been able to ask, as it was all confidential and involved tightly held trade secrets, a fact that had been emphasized nearly every day I had worked here.

But whatever the tech was, it worked. I'd been walking through this massive sheet of metal for nearly a week now. And when I had returned from lunch earlier in the day, even Dr. Schmidt's gray beard and mustache couldn't hide his grin as he declared in his thick accent that the project was a complete and unqualified success. Even though it was only Thursday, he gladly counted out my $1,000 completion bonus and had given me Friday off.

Everything was good ... at least until Jones started trying to kill me.

Although I had no idea what all the devices in the equipment room did, I knew it could turn that sheet of solid metal into something with no more resistance to my passing than thin air. That was fortunate because it was currently blocking my escape route. Repeating a series of steps I had witnessed many times, I flipped the appropriate switches and the racks of equipment started to emit the now-familiar hum. I took a run at the Environmental Barrier and the freedom beyond, hitting it square on at full speed.

I'm not sure, but I would guess that I bounced a full foot backward when I hit, feeling the fillings rattle in my teeth and seeing stars swirl in my vision.

Sometime during my headlong dash, Jones had apparently freed himself. He had entered the equipment room and was now nearly doubled over in laughter. I looked up at him from the floor, his muscled arms stretching the fabric of his black T-shirt.

"Jeremy ol' boy, you're gonna hurt yourself. Not that I much care, seeing how you slammed me to the floor under all that crap." And then, as if all my transgressions had become clear to him, his mouth curled into a sneer as he hissed, "Of course, I didn't much care for you before that either."

I shook my head in an attempt to clear it, only to double the pounding at my temples and the ringing in my ears. So, I closed my eyes, laid down face-first on the floor, and mentally shoved the anger and loathing from my mind. I had to think. What was wrong? The Barrier had worked perfectly earlier today. I was still trying to regain focus when Jones shouted, "Hey, quit stalling and get the hell back into the storeroom before I just shoot you here."

I turned my head and slowly pushed myself from the floor. But as I did, I noticed the data collection vest laying near a chair next to the wall. The vest, Dr. Schmidt had explained to me, was loaded with the electronics that were needed to collect information each time I passed through the Environmental Barrier. I had left it on the chair at the end of the last session; it must have fallen to the floor when I bounced off the plate.

Is it possible that the vest works with the equipment in this room?

It seemed the perfect security solution and security was everything on this project. If you had only the vest or only the equipment racks, you had nothing. You had to have both for the tech to work.

It was time to test my theory and my acting skills. I groaned softly and slowly dragged myself over to the chair, using it to raise myself to my knees. But in the process, I grabbed the vest and hit the power switch, as I shielded it from Jones's view under my body. I sensed the familiar low-level vibration.

Everything now felt right—the hum of the equipment rack in the background and the vibration in the vest hugged to my chest. I just needed to create some distance between myself and Jones in order to make one last attempt to gain my freedom.

While I wished that something more authoritative on the issue had come to mind, it didn't. What did spring unbidden to my thoughts was the Sandra Bullock movie, *Miss Congeniality*. According to it, the instep was quite sensitive and stomping on it could incapacitate someone, at least for a moment. And since I had not been sure at the time just exactly what the instep was, I had looked it up online. Obviously, now that I had done so, I was fully trained and well-prepared for what I was about to do.

Slowly, I got to my feet, still doubled over at the waist and holding the vest under my body. For his part, Jones seemed to be playing right into my hands as he stepped forward, grabbed my shoulder, and jerked me upright. But his mistake ended there, as he quickly stepped back. I don't know if he was expecting trouble or if this was just his normal defensive reaction, but he was nearly out of range. I dove forward anyway, aiming my heel at the inside of his foot.

I missed. But in the process, I had lunged so far that I had lost my balance. My other foot flew up as a counterweight as I fell backward and it caught Jones directly in the groin. I didn't need to recall the movie to know that area would work as well. He doubled over in agony.

I bounded for the Barrier. Feeling some unease from the first encounter, I slowed a bit before reaching it, but this time I passed through as if nothing was there.

Once in the reception room, I made straight for the front door and grabbed for the handle ... only to see my hand pass right through. For a split second, I stepped back, my mouth falling open, eyes wide.

Had the door been treated by the same processes that made the Environmental Barrier penetrable? Or was there no Barrier material, with a capital B? Was it all just everyday stuff—wood and plaster and metal and concrete? Surely, not everything in this room could have been treated making it temporarily vulnerable to the technology I was wearing and the contraptions in the backroom.

So, I stepped to an empty expanse of wall and cautiously walked forward. Almost before I knew it, I was standing outside the building. I spun around, staring at the wall I had just negotiated. The Barriers were not specially treated materials at all. The technology worked on anything, as long as I was in range of the equipment and was wearing the data collection vest.

I ran to my car, completely ignoring the pain and the pounding in my head. Shutting off the vest, I threw it in the back seat, leapt in, and started the engine. I knew exactly where I was headed as I raced down the street.

2. Cops and doughnuts

The population of metropolitan St. Louis is nearly three million people, but only about 320,000 of them live within the city limits. The rest have found homes in the almost too numerous to count townships, neighborhoods, and villages surrounding the city. Robertsville is one of them. It is located well south of downtown, situated atop the western bluffs of the Mississippi River. It is my home and the location where the research on the Environmental Barrier had taken place.

The Robertsville Police Station, however, was not the first stop as I had originally intended. Something about the bloody face staring back at me from my rearview mirror convinced me that a quick detour to a drug store, followed by some scrubbing and bandaging in their bathroom was in order. With that task out of the way, I entered the stationhouse, ready to turn the whole mess over to the police. I was ready to return to my quiet if somewhat dull life. Right now, dull sounded awfully good.

Everything went smoothly with the individual on the front desk, a sergeant, according to his introduction. He was throwing around terms like first-degree robbery and armed-criminal action, most of which meant little to me, but they sounded like something serious. He recorded a few of the basic facts—names, times, and locations. After waiting for maybe 25 minutes, the sergeant walked me back to meet with a detective.

"Jeremy Reynolds?" asked the individual at the desk. He was staring at a computer screen through his black, wire-rimmed glasses. "I'm Detective Vincent Underwood," he said without looking up.

The detective was small and wiry, with dark, close-cropped hair that was graying at the temples. His white shirt, tie, and jacket were probably standard work attire, although he seemed uncomfortable with them, pulling at his tie and cuffs repeatedly.

"Yes, I'm Jeremy. Nice to meet you."

"Likewise," Underwood said, as his eyes finally came away from the screen. But when they did, he grimaced, a shocked look spreading across his face. "Are you OK? Do you need to see a doctor?"

"No, I'm alright." Truthfully, I was still feeling every beat of my heart in my temples, but as somewhat of a klutz, this was familiar territory for me. "I just want to get this over with, go home, and get some sleep. It's been a long day."

"Are you sure you're alright?" I just nodded, which received a shrug from the detective in reply. "OK, please have a seat."

Underwood watched until I was comfortably settled in front of him; then, his gaze returned to the screen. "So, let me take a look at your background information." Occasionally, he muttered 'OK' or gave a nod, as his eyes traveled down the page.

"This 7212 number is a cell phone, right?"

"Correct," I said, patting the holster that hung from my belt. I knew holsters weren't the height of fashion, but butt-dialing and cracked screens had convinced me that they were stylish enough.

"No other phones? Work number? Landline?"

"Nope, no cable TV either. I've been cutting the cord." My comment was a bit off-topic for a question about having a landline, but wasn't this the trend? No lines. Have a cell. Stream video. Of course, I didn't actually stream video. The internet service that came with my apartment was much too slow. But there was one thing I liked about it—it fit my budgetary constraints perfectly. It was free.

"OK, sure," said Underwood. "Let's see. Three residences in the last two years." He paused to peer over the top of his glasses at me, then turned his attention back to the screen. "Robertsville for about six months. The Hill for about nine. And before that, nearly three years downtown. That downtown address sounds close to the ballpark."

"Yeah, Riley's place. It's close to Busch and has all the bells and whistles. Doorman, fitness center, pool, underground parking."

"Riley's place? Never heard of it."

"Oh, sorry, that's just what I call it. Riley was my girlfriend. It was really her idea to live there." Underwood looked at me for a moment, so I added, "We split up, so I moved on to more economically friendly accommodations."

After I spilled my guts about my ex-girlfriend and my just-above-the-poverty-line existence, I wasn't sure why I had. He hadn't asked about my personal life ... well, not about that part of it anyway. It was something about the gap he left in the conversation. I had to fill it with whatever popped into my head.

"So, you're relatively new to Robertsville."

It was a statement, not a question, but it still made me squirm a bit. Was I not qualified for his help? "Yeah, like you said. About six months."

Underwood continued his scan down the screen. "Let's see. For an emergency contact, you listed Ryan Reynolds in Denver."

"Yes, Uncle Ryan. No relation, no resemblance, if you're thinking of the movie star."

"Actually, I was thinking he's pretty far away. No one closer? No one in town?" asked Underwood.

"No. My parents are dead. I have an aunt in Nashville, which I guess is a bit closer."

"Probably something like 500 miles," said Underwood. Geography was never my strong suit, and I gave Underwood a what-can-I-say shrug.

"Well, if we're talking about emergencies, then Uncle Ryan's the right person. My aunt would just freak out, have a couple of stiff drinks, and then call my uncle." This quip didn't even warrant a smile from Underwood; he just nodded and typed something into his computer.

"It looks like you were with Frederickson and White until about two years ago, doing accounting work?"

"Yeah, mostly setting up accounting software systems, but I had an adding machine and kept a sharp pencil handy if the situation called for it." Thinking this bizarre claim would surely gain a chuckle from him, I was again disappointed. He just stared at me, deadpan.

As he worked, I leaned back in the chair, considering our chat thus far. Was I making a mistake, using my normal, somewhat sarcastic way of talking with Detective Underwood? Already, he thought my aunt was a lush and that I had some idea how to use an adding machine, when in fact, I'd only seen them in pictures. Maybe I should play this one by the book ... or at least, a little closer.

"That looks like it was almost two years ago," said Underwood. "Then, a string of temporary positions, none of which seem to involve accounting?" He gave me that questioning look over his wire-rims again.

"Yes, I've been taking some time off."

After I had quit my job, I had tried out different socially acceptable excuses for just not caring about work anymore. I almost went with, 'I'm taking some time to find myself.' It had a nice, vague ring to it and it implied some interest in self-improvement even if I had none. But in the past, it had elicited a continuous stream of recommendations for everything from career counselors to psychics and so, I had moved on to 'I'm on sabbatical.' The trouble with it was that everyone seemed to think you had to be in academia to take one. I wasn't sure about that, but I didn't have time to change public opinion just so I could cover my lack of interest in work.

But one thing I never tried was a real explanation for my disinterest in a career. That would require that I explore and understand my motivations and I just didn't care enough to make the effort.

"OK, I think that pretty well covers your background. That's all just a formality, reference information, in case we need it. I'd like to go through the incident report now. It looks like you have been working for a Dr. Johannes Schmidt on some type of market research study at 7677 East Collingsway for the last five weeks."

"Correct. Lots of temp work is anything from an hour or two to maybe a week. Sometimes, it's not on location at all. It's take these three bottles of soda home, drink them, and write down what you think. So, I was really lucky when this five-week job came along."

"And you finished it today, on Thursday?"

"Correct. I guess technically, it wasn't a full five weeks. We finished a day early, around 4 o'clock and Dr. Schmidt paid me a completion bonus. A thousand dollars. Then, he left, and his associate, Thomas Jones, asked me to review a bunch of the notes I had written earlier for the study. Just what I'd observed, stuff like that. And I initialed each one if it looked OK to me. That seemed ... oh, nothing." I broke off, thinking that I was starting to ramble.

But Underwood said, "No, go ahead. It seemed what?"

"It seemed like busywork. I couldn't remember anything today that I hadn't remembered when I wrote the notes the first time. It seemed pointless."

"You continued that until about 5:30 when Jones assaulted you and attempted to steal the bonus money. Is that right?" asked Underwood.

"Yeah, it was about that time." I paused and closed my eyes, trying to recall the exact conversation. "Actually, I said something like, this couldn't be about the bonus. And he said you have no idea."

Underwood sat back in his chair and rubbed the back of his neck. "That seems a little vague, doesn't it? Like it could mean something else ... even the opposite of him wanting to steal the money?"

Now, it was my turn to ponder the exchange. "I hadn't thought of it that way … but you could be right," I admitted. I wished I had reviewed the attack in my mind before coming in.

"You also indicated that he took a shot at you?" The inflection in his voice made it clear this was a question.

"Yes." Detective Underwood sat looking at me. "Yeah, I know. It seems strange that anyone would try to kill someone over a thousand dollars." I stopped, realizing that he'd done it to me again with his fill-in-the-silence ploy.

"Maybe," Underwood said. "There are situations that can make people desperate for money." He paused, stroking his chin. "Did your job pay well? I mean, for temporary work?"

"Well, I was having some trouble coming up with the down payment on that vacation home in the Cayman Islands, but yeah, it paid OK." Still seeing no reaction from the detective, I finished with the details he probably really wanted. "I was making $500 a week, before the bonus."

"And Jones worked for Dr. Schmidt?"

A frown crossed my face. To me, the implication was that if Schmidt paid his temps well, surely the associate would be making good money. And with good pay, there was no reason for Jones to rob me. But if this was what Underwood was fishing for, why ask me? All of this would be answered as soon as he talked to Schmidt. He would be able to quote Jones's salary to the penny, talk about their association, discuss whether Jones had a history as a hitman, whatever.

Deciding that Underwood had to know all of this, I just said, "Yes, Jones worked for Schmidt."

"Was there ever any indication that Jones was on drugs?"

Good, at least Underwood was headed back to issues that would support my robbery theory. If Jones was on drugs, he might be desperate enough, and perhaps strung out enough to come gunning for me. There was just one problem with that explanation.

"No, I can't say that I noticed anything like that," I said. "If anything, he just seemed bored to tears. If he was using drugs, he was buying the wrong stuff." More typing by Underwood followed.

"Your injuries, the bandage on your forehead, the bruise, all the scrapes and such. Are any of those gunshot wounds or the result of Jones hitting you?"

"No."

"So, they are all self-inflicted?" asked Underwood.

I didn't like the sound of that, even if it was technically true, and sat up a bit straighter in my chair. "I got them from trying to get away from Jones," I said evenly. "The cuts and scrapes on my arms and legs are mostly from when the shelves in the storeroom fell. That's in the report."

At that moment, an officer walked by. As he dropped a piece of paper on Underwood's desk, the officer said, "Cleveland's a go. Time's on the pink slip." And he walked away.

As Underwood picked up the note to read it, he said, "Yeah, I saw the report ... climbing up there to hide."

I uncrossed my legs and slid to the edge of my chair, my face going warm with his words. If Underwood was implying something about me, I needed to clear the air. Macho posturing against a guy with a gun was nuts in my opinion.

The detective finished reading and dropped the note on his desk. When his eyes came back to mine, he said, "Yeah, that was a clever bit of maneuvering in the storeroom. If you hadn't thought your way out of it, I'd probably be interviewing you from a hospital room. Or not at all."

I slumped back, opening my mouth to speak but nothing came out, until finally, I managed, "Thanks. Best I could come up with, on the spot."

Underwood tented his fingers in front of his face, his eyes closed for a moment. Then, he asked, "The knot on your forehead—it's pretty nasty. Did you get that when the shelves collapsed?"

"Um, not exactly." I swallowed, searching for the right words. "I got it from running into a door when I was trying to get into the reception area."

Wrinkling his brow, Underwood asked, "You missed the door handle and ran into it?"

"Well ... it was more like I thought the door was open but it wasn't," I said slowly, searching for the right words.

Underwood rubbed his chin again. "You thought it was open? You mean, you thought it was unlocked but it wasn't?"

"Yeah, more or less."

I studied the papers on Underwood's desk, not wanting to look him in the eye. I wasn't prepared to say I thought the equipment was on and then nearly splattered my brains all over the lab when it wasn't. He wouldn't believe my story about the technology anyway, so why give him an excuse to drop the whole case?

Underwood sighed, apparently resigned that I wasn't going to explain further. "Did you lose consciousness when you hit the door?"

"If I did, it wasn't long."

"Any problems with dizziness or delusions since then?" he asked.

"No."

I tried for a touch of defiance in my voice, certain he was implying that much of my tale was a hallucination. I thought about saying I was positive the incident was real, but if it was an illusion, my certainty it happened would just be part of the misperception anyway. But the circularity of the argument made my head spin so I kept quiet. And besides, all of these questions would disappear as soon as Underwood got to the lab anyway.

"So, what were they studying at this lab on Collingsway? Was there anything important in the study?"

"Yeah, I'd say so," I said, grinning internally at what I considered an enormous understatement from the detective. Earth-shattering, life-altering, or mind-blowing were all more appropriate adjectives than 'important.' Underwood waited, but I wasn't going to fill the silence this time.

"You told the sergeant you couldn't talk about the research there because of confidentiality reasons," said Underwood. "But it might really help with the case if I knew what was going on."

I hesitated, debating the alternatives in my mind. Finally, I took a deep breath and prepared myself to disappoint him. "I'm sorry, Detective, but I'm just not sure I should say more. Dr. Schmidt was really serious about security and had me sign all kinds of legal documents. He said all their research involved industrial secrets and that I could be fined, even put in jail for describing anything about it. Look, I'm certain as soon as you talk to Dr. Schmidt, he'll fill you in on the details of his work and everything he knows about Jones."

"Hopefully, but so far, we're having trouble finding anyone by the name of Schmidt associated with the Collingsway address."

"Well, he wouldn't be there now," I said, smiling because he had made such an obvious error. "It's after hours." But as soon as I said it, I realized that the police must have done more than just a drive-by to say they were having a hard time finding him.

"That's not exactly what I meant," said Underwood, confirming my thoughts. "We've contacted the owner of the building. He has no record of a Dr. Schmidt or a Mr. Jones. His records show a different name for the tenant. Of course, it's possible that someone else rented the property for Dr. Schmidt and we're checking into that name as well."

"No record of them," I mumbled. I ran my hand through my hair, my mind racing through the possibilities. "That's all really strange, but what about just contacting the company where Dr. Schmidt works? They'll know how you can get a hold of him."

"I was just getting ready to ask about the company," said Underwood. "You said the name was ...." He paused, checking the computer screen. "Environmental Building Materials Research, Inc., right?"

I leaned back and stretched my legs, releasing some tension I hadn't really noticed until now. We were back on indisputable ground. "Yes, that's right. The entire reception area was covered with posters and brochures about them."

Underwood cocked an eye at me and asked, "Not Sustainable Building Materials Company?"

"No, absolutely not," I said firmly. "I saw the name nearly every day for more than a month. I'm certain it was Environmental Building Materials Research."

Underwood drew a long breath, then released it. "Well, we haven't found such a company yet. There's no business even close to that name in St. Louis and none with an exact match anywhere in the country."

My fingertips went to my temples, perhaps preparing for the headache that was already bad becoming much worse if things kept going this way. "What does that mean?"

"Maybe nothing. It could be his own company and too new to be listed online. Or he may have made it up, to give the study more legitimacy, make people feel comfortable being there. By the way, was the name of the company on the ad for the temporary position?"

"The ad, yeah. I could make a quick call to ...." But I stopped mid-sentence, realizing I was wrong.

"Call to who?" asked Underwood.

"I was going to say that I could call Ableton Temp Services, which is the agency that I mostly use. They could answer that question. But for the job with Schmidt, I didn't go through them. I found a notice on a bulletin board at that grocery store on Fifth Street. You know which one I mean?"

"Yeah, sure, I stop there for doughnuts once and awhile."

I wasn't sure if he was trying to be the straight man for a joke about cops and doughnuts, but given his track record on humor to this point, I decided not. And besides, while my uncle who is a county sheriff jokes about it all the time, I think you need to be part of the fraternity to do that, and I wasn't. Finally, I just nodded and filled the silence with,

"Yeah, they have all kinds of stuff on that bulletin board—garage sales, jobs, auctions, you name it."

"And was the name of the company on the ad?"

I chuckled. "Oh, yeah, that was the question, wasn't it?" I closed my eyes in concentration as if I might be able to wring the memory from my brain cells if I squeezed my eyelids hard enough. "Sorry, but I'm not sure. That was a long time ago."

"Yes, it was. What else do you remember about the ad?" asked Detective Underwood. "I mean, did it have those tear-off tabs with the phone number or did you have to write the number down. Did it describe the work? Was there a picture of their lab?"

"No tear-off tabs. I remember writing the number on the grocery receipt I had. No pictures, just an address .... Hey, wait a minute," I said, as I sat bolt upright. "The name of the company wasn't given. I remember now. I was going to check out who I'd be working for online before I went in, but it didn't say."

"So, you only saw the name of the company inside the building on Collingsway?"

I didn't respond at first, still slowly shaking my head in awe at how he had dragged that memory out of the recesses of my mind. Maybe it was just police interrogation 101 for him, but I was impressed. When my thoughts caught up to his last question, I said, "Yeah, I guess that's right. The only place I saw the name was in the lab."

Underwood nodded slowly, as he rubbed the back of his neck with his hand. "You know, Jeremy, this dead-end on the company is why I hoped you would tell me what he was doing. If I knew that, I'd know where to start checking."

I continued to hesitate, so he asked, "Would it help if I looked into building material research?"

"Ah, maybe … but I doubt it," I stammered. "Look, I'm really sorry, but until we're out of options to find him, I'd rather not talk about the research. I don't know, but everything I signed looked official."

Underwood shrugged, saying, "Well, we're not far away from being out of options now. So, be thinking about it." He was making it hard to think of anything else.

"Let's see, your physical description of Thomas Jones," continued Underwood. "Male, late 20s or early 30s, about six foot three, 220 pounds, wavy brown hair, brown eyes, muscular build, no tattoos or other distinguishing marks." He looked at me over his wire-rims.

"Yeah, I know, that could fit a lot of people," I admitted. "That could be me, subtract a couple of inches in height and 35 pounds in weight. Oh, and darken and straighten the hair." Muscular wasn't totally accurate either, as lanky was probably closer, but I didn't see the need to say that.

"Is there anything else you can add to his description?"

My eyes roamed the room as if I was hoping to find a photo of him on one of the walls. What could I say about Jones? He was just a regular looking guy. I got a temporary reprieve when the detective's phone rang.

"Underwood," he said as he picked it up, followed by "Yeah," "When," and finally, "No, now." It was not the most illuminating conversation from just his side. When he hung up, his eyes returned to me as if asking, 'anything?'

"He often looked like he needed a shave. But that's about all I can think of," I said, as my voice trailed off.

More nodding, more typing. Then, the detective asked, "Other than Schmidt and Jones, did you see anyone else at the lab?"

"No, I don't think so. It seemed like a small operation with some really tight security and some pretty incredible tech."

"Technology that you can't tell me about?" said Underwood. I frowned, and he waved his hand as if saying, 'forget I asked.'

"So, do you realize you were working for John Smith and Tom Jones?" asked Underwood.

I frowned, saying, "What ... hold on a second. It was Tom Jones, but the other guy ... the doctor who ran the research was Johannes Schmidt."

"Same thing. Johannes Schmidt is a German name, which would be John Smith in the States."

"Ah ... John Smith. Are you sure about that?" I stared down at Underwood's desk, wondering what this might possibly mean. "Well, I guess common names are common for a reason," I offered weakly.

"Perhaps," Detective Underwood replied. His phone rang again and I was treated to another one-sided call. "Underwood," "No," "When," and finally, "Good."

When he hung up, he said, "I'm meeting the owner of the building on Collingsway and someone from the community college. The school rents the storeroom," Underwood explained. "Given the nature of this incident, you're welcome to meet me there if you want. But you need to do exactly what I say if you go."

"Now?" It was probably only about 8:00, but apparently dodging bullets is tiring. After considering his offer further, however, I said, "Yeah, sure. I just didn't expect it to happen this fast."

"It doesn't always work this way, but both these people are available. We've had a car at the Collingsway building for about the last half hour, but my guy can't sit there all night. And frankly, we don't have enough to break down the door and take a look. So, you're lucky that these two parties are willing to come by now."

"Great, I'll meet you there," I said.

"Good, and if we get there before the other two, you can tell me more about how good you are on an adding machine," said Underwood. "Or a slide rule, if you have one of those."

I chuckled as I stood to leave. What do you know? Beneath Detective Vincent Underwood's 'just the facts' exterior was a sense of humor.

3. Here today ...

When I pulled up to the lab, two individuals were standing outside and Detective Underwood was just parking his car. As I joined them all on the sidewalk, Underwood asked, "Mr. Santiago?"

"Yes," said one of the two men, and offered his hand.

"Mr. Cleveland?" The second man nodded and they shook hands as well.

I was feeling a bit like a fifth wheel when Underwood turned to me and finished the introductions. "Gentlemen, this is Mr. Jeremy Reynolds, the victim in this alleged incident. Mr. Santiago owns the property and Mr. Cleveland is from the community college."

Cleveland winced when he looked at my face, but Santiago seemed unaffected.

"I'm so sorry about what happened to you," said Santiago, as I caught up on the handshakes. "I hope you are alright." His condolences had the ring of an oft-practiced phrase, which would make sense if he owned much property in this area. The term crime-ridden was perhaps too strong, but 'rough' seemed an appropriate description of the neighborhood.

"Thank you. I'm fine. I'd just like to see the guy caught," I said.

Both men nodded in agreement, as Santiago added, "Yeah, too many criminals on the street." He took a sideways glance at Underwood as if realizing that the detective might take exception to his remark.

If Underwood did, you couldn't tell it from his voice. "Well, let's take a look inside."

As Santiago unlocked the door and swung it open, I gasped, my eyes going wide at what I saw—or more correctly, at what I didn't see. The first room, nominally the reception area, was empty, except for a desk and a single chair. Gone was all the promotional literature that had been on display in one bookcase and spread across another library table. Missing were the posters hung from every wall that declared the Environmental Building Materials Research company the future savior of our planet. Absent were the charts and graphs showing ... well, I didn't remember exactly what they showed. But they were colorful and attention-grabbing and now, they were gone, as were all of the other chairs and tables that had been in this area.

Santiago looked around the room, then turned to Detective Underwood and shrugged. "Yeah, everything looks fine. It looks like it did when I rented it to him." I must have looked stricken when he glanced at me, because he quickly added, "We just rent it semi-furnished."

"Well, Jeremy?" asked the detective, turning to me.

"No, this isn't the same. Not at all," I said, the words flying out of my mouth. I proceeded to go through the room, detailing just what had been where, the last time I had seen it—a table here, a poster there, two chairs in that corner.

Underwood was jotting notes in a small book he carried with him. Santiago, on the other hand, was staring at me, arms folded across his chest.

When I got to the door between reception and the equipment lab, I said, "One of the biggest differences is right here. When I was here, this door was the Environmental Barrier. It was the material they were studying."

Evidently, Santiago couldn't listen any longer, as he thrust himself between me and the door. "They could have put all kinds of pictures and papers in here. I wouldn't know. That's their business. But all those tables and chairs? They're not mine. And the door? This is the only door that's ever been here," he protested as if I had been questioning his honesty.

"No, sorry, Mr. Santiago," I said. "I'm sure you're right. This is the original door, but they had taken it off the hinges and put the test door here. This door was in the next room, leaning up against the wall in a corner." Santiago continued to scowl at me.

Underwood ignored our exchange, going directly for the issue that apparently remained at the top of his mind. "And what was this door like?" he asked.

"It changed ... as the study went along," I said slowly, glancing around the audience and seeing nothing but puzzled looks. But I wasn't going to explain further, at least not yet and certainly not in front of all these strangers. It would be bad enough to describe the research to the police, but all these civilians? No way.

"OK," said the detective. "Can we see the next room?"

When Santiago opened the door to what I had known as the equipment lab, the story was the same. The racks of computer equipment, a device that looked like an antenna, the power supplies—they were all gone. And like before, Santiago confirmed everything that was originally in the room was still there.

Giving another slow, disbelieving shake of my head, I itemized all I could remember of this area. When I had finished, Detective Underwood turned to Santiago. "On the phone, you said you thought the individual renting these two rooms was Jose Verde. Did you check?"

"Yes, and that's correct."

Underwood just stared for a moment, but Santiago seemed to have nothing to add. So, he asked, "And Jose Verde would be Joe Green, in Spanish?"

"I guess," replied Santiago evenly.

"Seems like a fairly common alias, doesn't it?" asked Underwood.

Santiago shrugged, palms up. "Hey, I get a John Doe, from time to time. So what? He never complained. And he paid in cash, right up through last month when he moved out."

"He moved out last month?" I blurted, turning to Santiago. Underwood glared at me, as I had obviously forgotten his 'follow my lead' warning.

"That's what I said," replied Santiago, staring back at me. I had the feeling that if Underwood hadn't been there, that statement would have been followed with, 'you hard of hearing or what?'

Underwood intervened. "Did you come by your property any time this month to verify that?"

"No, like I told you—or maybe I told the other person I talked to on the phone—I was out of town, on vacation. I just got home to your phone call earlier tonight. But Mr. Verde said he was leaving at the end of the month. And he didn't pay for this month; I checked my locking mailbox when I got home. Obviously, he's gone," Santiago said, putting considerable emphasis on the word, 'obviously.'

"Did anyone know you would be gone on vacation?" asked Underwood.

"All my tenants knew."

I looked down at the ground, slowly shaking my head. This information was concerning. Verde/Jones hadn't paid rent covering the last 10 days, much less today. So, if he and Schmidt had been using the property, they would be taking a chance. Why risk getting caught for a month's rent? And why would Schmidt have gone along with a plan like this? Maybe he didn't know? Maybe Jones was desperate enough for money that he had pocketed the rent and not told Schmidt.

There was, of course, another possibility and my frown deepened when I forced myself to consider it. I was still certain about the room and the study. I had been here daily for over a month and had $1,000 in my pocket as proof. But what if the study had ended 10 days ago? What if Schmidt had paid me, Jones had said goodbye, and I had done ... whatever I did for the last week and a half. Then, today, I hit my head, but not in the lab. Not while fleeing from Jones. But somewhere else. Maybe I had tripped over a rug at my apartment. Clearly, my tidiness had suffered, right along with my interest in the future.

I tried to massage the tension from my forehead. If this was true, then the memory of Jones chasing me around the lab shooting at me was nothing but a delusion. The rest of the blood and bruises were real enough; there was no way to deny them. But maybe they were, as Underwood had put it, self-inflicted. I thought everything had been real, but my confidence was slipping. Who knew what fantasies might emerge after a blow to the head?

At least Underwood was still digging, and I forced my thoughts back to his voice as he addressed Santiago. "Do you have a forwarding address for Verde?"

I thought Santiago came close to rolling his eyes; maybe all of his business was cash only, ask-not, tell-not. In the end, he just said, "No."

Underwood nodded, then said, "OK, let's take a look at the storeroom." I was expecting Mr. Cleveland, as the representative of the community college to step forward and unlock the door, but it was Santiago who started toward it. Evidently, I wasn't the only one who was surprised.

"Hold on a second," said Underwood. "Mr. Cleveland, don't you have a key to this door?"

"Oh, no, not this door. There's another door, on the other side of the building that we use. Once we get inside, you'll see it."

I suspected that Underwood already knew this, but just in case, I said, "Jones and I came in this way." He nodded. If Jones had used a key, it hadn't come from anyone from the school.

"Mr. Santiago, besides yourself, who has a key to this door?"

"Well, no one. There's never been a reason to give anyone a key for this door because no one has ever rented all three rooms."

Underwood looked at the lock. If he saw evidence it had been picked, he said nothing. Then, he stepped aside and said, "Please go ahead and open it."

Santiago obliged, and when he swung the door open, I took an involuntary step backward, gawking at the contents inside. Here, the problem was the opposite from before; this room held much more than I remembered.

"Well, Mr. Cleveland?" asked Detective Underwood, nodding toward the room, the meaning of the question apparently obvious to both men.

"It looks fine," he replied simply.

I peered through the open door, my eyes traveling around the room as I slowly shook my head in disbelief. "Are you certain ... I mean ... isn't there stuff in here you don't recognize?" I stammered. True, I had only been in here for a few minutes, but the empty area just inside the door was now piled high with furniture and computers.

Cleveland glanced through the door again, then said, "Maybe, but I don't think so. I don't get in here much. No one does, but everything seems OK."

We all stepped into the storeroom, although there was hardly space for the four of us. "What about those computers right over there?" I pointed to a set that I was fairly certain had been in the lab. "Does the community college own them?"

Cleveland looked offended as if I was accusing the school of theft. "I'm sure they do. I don't remember that specific set, but the ones right beside them. They belonged to Dr. Fredrick in Sociology. I only remember because he had one of the early class voting systems and you can still see the buttons right there. The rest, I could look up … if the detective needs that information."

My eyes continued to dart around the room, searching for something that had to be unique to Schmidt's research. "What about that thing that looks like an antenna of some sort?"

"Sure. That was Billy Gibson's crop monitoring system. He set up sensors in some cornfields and collected data on things like moisture and nutrients in the soil. State of the art stuff, 15 years ago. Now, you probably couldn't give it away." He laughed, then went a little red, realizing he had probably said more than he should.

"OK, but what about that big metal plate?" I was starting to sound desperate, even to myself. But in a roomful of furniture and electronics, the last Environmental Barrier was clearly out of place. Surely it was something that Jones and Schmidt had acquired solely for the research.

Cleveland drew back from me slightly as if I had some form of mental condition that might be contagious. "We used it the same way everybody does—to cover street repairs. But with budget cuts, there's less of that. The plate's surplus property—just like everything else in this room."

"Surplus property? This is all surplus equipment?" I asked, rubbing my forehead.

Unease flitted across Cleveland's face, as he nodded slowly. "Yes, of course. What did you think it was?"

I didn't answer, taking a deep breath and wandering around the stacks of furniture and electronics to look more closely. The first thing I came to was one of the tables that had been in reception. I was certain it had been there. But as I bent closer, I had to admit that without the colorful graphs and brochures artfully spread across its top, it looked tired and worn.

Then, I approached a rack of computer equipment that seemed familiar. I had never noticed before, but the rack had wheels on the bottom; it would be easy to move. And in its current context, without the hum and blinking lights and without Schmidt scurrying around twisting knobs and turning dials, it looked antiquated and frankly ... not very realistic. Somehow, the shabby setting of the storeroom seemed to have stripped the electronic gear of its high-tech sheen.

"But how did he do it with all this old junk," I mumbled to no one in particular.

Cleveland responded anyway. "How did he do what?"

I just waved my hand, too confused to answer. Nothing was making sense. I closed my eyes, hoping to block out the world for a moment and see if there was any puzzle in which these strange pieces fit. Obviously, some of this equipment belonged to the school. Cleveland could hardly be wrong about all of it. But was the real tech scattered in here? That seemed impossible. I mean, how could Schmidt/Jones be certain the community college wouldn't throw open the storeroom doors one day for a garage sale? Or that they wouldn't donate everything to an elementary school if anyone would take it? So, if the real technology wasn't in here ....

I slapped my forehead, momentarily forgetting about my injury. The searing pain reminded me as I cradled my head in my hands a moment till the stars dissipated. I turned to Underwood and Cleveland. "I think what Schmidt did was to hide his technology in plain sight. He took some of the equipment from here to put in his lab. That way, anyone who got a glance wouldn't know what was real and what was junk."

I immediately regretted my choice of words, but Cleveland didn't seem offended. "He stole some of our equipment to use in his lab?" Cleveland glanced at Underwood, whose attention was focused on me, a frown on his face.

"Well, borrowed," I said. "He borrowed it, as a distraction. It was just part of his security ...." My voice trailed off, as Underwood continued to scowl at me.

To this point, Underwood had always seemed prepared to entertain just about any hypothesis, however, improbable. So, I gained some insight into what he thought of my current notion when he said, "Hmm, I'm not sure, Jeremy. It seems a bit ... over the top to break in here and move a bunch of equipment just to hide what he's working on."

My face fell.

"Although, I guess it's possible," Underwood said slowly. I wondered if he made that concession just so I wouldn't shut down. "If that's the case, do you have any idea what's missing? What was in the lab, but not in here now?"

As I looked at the tangled pile of boxes and cords, cables and displays, screens and disk drives, my spirits dropped. I hung my head, talking to the floor. "No, sorry, I could never be certain. There was so much stuff in the lab. And even if I remembered some gizmo for sure, I wouldn't know what it was anyway."

I suspected that none of his Interrogation 101 tricks would help me remember anything this complex. It looked like I was right, as Underwood nodded and turned toward Santiago and Cleveland. "Gentlemen, it's late. I really appreciate you coming out at this hour, but I think it's time Mr. Reynolds and I leave you to lock up. I'll be in contact if anything more comes up." They all shook hands and started for the door.

I was too dejected for pleasantries and just stood there, staring at the room. Beyond the pile of equipment from the lab, the shelves lined the walls, filled with the latest technology from a bygone era, just as I remembered them. Even the old desk lamp that I had tripped over was laying in the aisle. There was the occasional scrap of wood or fragment of a shattered piece of electronics where the shelves had collapsed, but this was evidence of nothing. The same type of debris littered the floor on the other side of the room, in an area we had never been. Everything was exactly as it had been when Jones and I had entered the storeroom ... except for one thing.

"Detective, I know where a bullet is," I announced.

"What?" Underwood asked, spinning back to look at me.

"I said, I know where we can recover a bullet that Jones shot at me. Right here." And I stretched out my arm, pointing to a spot on the support column. "Can we dig it out?"

Underwood leaned closer, looking at the spot I had indicated. "It seems pretty small for a bullet. But there is a repair here, and it looks recent. I don't suppose you would know why a spot on this column has been recently plastered, would you, Mr. Santiago?"

"No, not really. I haven't been back here in months. Maybe the school?"

"Well, like I said, we come in a different door, over there," Cleveland said, as he pointed toward the exit sign across the room. "So, not many people from the school would get all the way back here. But yeah, sometimes the companies we get to move equipment nick up the walls and the school has been known to patch them. But I can't be certain about this specific spot."

"Well, the only way I could dig it out would be to get a court order and that would take time. That is unless Mr. Santiago wants to approve it now," said Underwood, looking around the edge of his glasses at the landlord.

Santiago shrugged. "I have no problem with that, but someone would have to pay for the repair."

"I'll pay," I said, just a little too quickly. Then, more cautiously, I asked, "Just how much would something like that cost?"

"Oh, I don't know. Maybe, $200 would cover it," replied Santiago.

"For a dimple?" I said as I stared at the spot. Santiago just shrugged. "OK, whatever," I conceded. "I just want this over with."

Underwood pulled a knife out of his pocket and started working on the spot. "I suppose forensics will give me hell if there is a slug down there and I scratch it up. I'll go in slowly."

And he did, shaving off tiny layers, one after another. But even so, it was only about five minutes when he announced, "I'm to the bottom. Nothing. In fact, not much of a hole. If a bullet hit here, it just glanced off."

I looked where it might have traveled if it ricocheted off the column and found myself staring at a pile of furniture that went half-way to the ceiling. I just shook my head, pulled two one-hundred-dollar bills from my wallet, and handed them to Santiago. I figured that should cover the 50-cents of spackling he'd probably put there if he ever got around to doing anything at all.

When we went outside, Santiago and Cleveland said their good-byes to Detective Underwood, and Santiago locked the door. I was too frustrated to know or care if they even looked my way, and soon the detective and I were the only ones left, standing under the light at the entrance to the lab.

"OK, Jeremy," Underwood said, looking me in the eye. "This is where the rubber meets the road. Yes, you were definitely injured. But finding out who and why seems to boil down to finding Schmidt or Jones or the company Schmidt works for. But that's going to be nearly impossible with what I have because what I have is nothing. So, what's this industrial secret, because frankly, without that, I don't even know where to start."

I looked down, absentmindedly rubbing my hands on the front of my jeans. I didn't know what to do. If I didn't tell Underwood, he would close the case. If I did, he might close it anyway. It was not like what I had to say was going to be easy for him to swallow.

But let's say he believed me. Then, he might find Schmidt. And if he did, Jones would go to jail. But I might go to jail, too. A judge or jury might have sympathy, given all I had been through, but maybe not. Maybe industrial spying is one of those crimes where they lock the door and throw away the key. I had no idea.

I kicked idly at a pebble laying near my foot, having decided to stay quiet and let Jones go. I wasn't happy about it, but there were too many ways this situation could go wrong. But when I opened my mouth to tell Underwood, I heard myself say, "Can you keep this confidential?" If Jones continued his homicidal ways, I didn't want to know that I might have been able to stop him but hadn't tried.

"If at all possible, yes. But I can't be in a position where I'm breaking the law."

"Sure, I understand that." I collected my thoughts, then started, "Dr. Schmidt was making a device that lets people pass through a door, but without opening it or letting anything else through."

Underwood's eyes narrowed, as he rubbed the back of his neck. "I'm not sure I understand. He's working on some sort of high-tech door that seals right behind you? Maybe it has something like those collision detectors on cars, so it slams shut just as your foot clears? Something like that?"

"No, not exactly," I said slowly. I tried to rub the creases from my forehead, realizing what a monumental leap of faith I was asking of him. "The door is solid. But with this equipment, you can walk right through it. And after you get through, nothing else can pass."

Underwood stared at me blankly and asked, "And you said these doors are solid?"

"Yeah. Apparently, it works with anything—plastic, wood, metal, whatever. At the end of the study, we were using that big metal plate we saw in the storeroom."

"The road plate? The thing that probably weighs a ton? You could walk right through it, but nothing else could?" Again, his face was a mask. He didn't seem surprised or upset. He spoke like he just wanted to check the facts.

"Yeah, not after I get beyond it. It's back to being a solid slab of metal. Unbelievable, huh?" I said rapidly, relieved that I had finally been able to confide in someone.

Underwood looked away and stood staring into the night. When he returned his gaze to me, he said, "I'll keep the case open and call if any new leads come up."

"What?" My voice was a bit louder than I intended. "I was almost killed earlier today. You can't just let Jones go, now that I've told you what Dr. Schmidt was building."

Underwood reached out and put his hand on my shoulder. I nearly threw it off in my anger but realized that in his place, I would be skeptical too. I waited. When Underwood spoke, his voice was calm and quiet. "Jeremy, you seem like a nice guy. Maybe a bit aimless ... and obviously, a lot confused. Go see a doctor about your head. You may be worse off than you think."

His words shook me, and I swallowed hard, trying to believe my reality was intact.

Then, Underwood continued. "Second, if you are OK, you need to let this go. If you don't, there are laws against wasting the time of a law enforcement official. People don't walk through solid metal plates, and if you keep claiming they do .... Well, I'd hate to see you get into trouble. Now go home and get some sleep."

There was nothing I could do. I couldn't convince Underwood of my claims by walking through a wall. By now, I was certain that Schmidt or Jones had the real components and had left nothing but the trash in the storeroom. I dropped my head and stumbled toward my car.

I drove away, thinking that even though Jones was going free, I had tried. And he'd probably leave me alone, if for no other reason than I was already down to $800. That is, if it was the money he was really after.

4. Peeping Jeremy

When I left the now-deserted lab, my body got into an argument with itself. Food or sleep? Sleep or food? Realizing that my stomach and muscles were never going to agree, I got my head involved. Going to bed this hungry would probably result in tossing and turning for hours. I might zone out for a while, but my rest would be troubled, and I would wake up with racking hunger pangs. OK, maybe my head was being a bit melodramatic, but I'd be hungry. The alternative, while perhaps not pleasant, sounded better. I'd force my eyes open for the next hour, chow down, and then sleep until noon. My head made a convincing argument for the latter, and I stopped by a 24-hour Mexican restaurant, well known for quantity at low cost.

After getting my food—four, one-dollar burritos—I drove home and parked in front of my one-bedroom apartment. My building was one of the oldest in Robertsville and had been a single-family home. I had never been able to get a feel for the original owner, although one thing was clear; he had grandiose plans for his domicile. It was laid out in the center-hall style, found in the mansions and mini-mansions of the 1904 St. Louis World's Fair homes. But where these grand old homes on Westmoreland and Portland

Place were 10,000 square feet and upwards, my building was about 1,800. And then, it had been made into a duplex.

By itself, the decision to divide the residence wasn't necessarily a bad one; the execution of it, however, doomed the building. First, the owner had placed the entrance to the lower floor, which was my apartment, beside the original door. The first door had been centered on the front of the house, so the new entry left the building with a strange, lopsided look. The new door opened to a short hall that served the living room and terminated in the kitchen. The space for the hall had been taken from the living room, meaning that it went from being small to being microscopic. And because the hall ended at the kitchen, one had to go through the kitchen and the bathroom to get to the bedroom.

But the owner's nightmare of a floorplan was my dream of low-cost accommodations. I was living in my apartment for a song.

Running across the front of the house was a porch, its roof held up by metal posts that had long ago replaced the wooden columns that would have originally graced a home of this style. But even in its current state, it was one of my favorite spots. I grabbed my sack of burritos from the seat of the car, retrieved the data collection vest from the trunk, and dumped both of them on a comfortable, but well-worn chair I kept out front. Then, I made the trek down the hall to the kitchen, came back with a beer, and settled in for my late-night dinner.

It was still unseasonably warm for November in St. Louis, but even so, the temperature was dropping as the hour approached 1:00 AM. I hadn't thought to grab a jacket, so I just slipped on the data collection vest. It wasn't the warmest or the most comfortable, but it would do. I planned to make short work of the burritos anyway.

After all the hassles of the last half-day, the night was making up for it. There was a full moon and in the low-level light it provided, I could just make out the bright red leaves of the maple trees as they joined the greens, yellows, and oranges of their compatriots. The leaves that still clung to the trees made a soft, rustling sound as a slight breeze played through the branches. About the only other sounds were the occasional bark of a dog in the distance or the sound of a car blocks away. It was all very serene, all very peaceful.

As I finished my third burrito, I was thinking of putting the fourth in the refrigerator. The thought of sleep was becoming overpowering. I wouldn't even need to set an alarm. However long I might sleep, it would endanger no plans because I had none. I didn't have to go to work; I was between jobs if you could say that about temp positions. I didn't need to meet anyone; no one was waiting for me to regale them with my latest stories. I thought my routine would eventually change, but for now, it was an easy life that revolved around necessities rather than ambitions and obligations. And right now, the necessity was for sleep.

"Drowsy there, Jeremy ol' boy?" came the familiar, sing-song voice out of the darkness. I jerked upright, as every muscle in my body tensed. Staring into the night, I could just make out Jones's muscular frame, silhouetted by the street light behind him. My heart started thundering in my chest.

"What the hell do you want, Jones?" I asked, biting off each word. "I've been to the police. They know all about you. They have your name."

"Oh, you've been to the police, Jeremy," he replied, continuing his melodious, mocking tone. "But what I don't know is, do they think you're one of those raving conspiracy theorists because you didn't spill your guts about the study? Or do they think you're just plain looney because you did? And just what name did you give them, anyway?"

I sat forward, knocking the last burrito to the porch as the refried beans splattered across the boards. I clutched the arms of the chair so tightly that the wood creaked. "They're watching. Anything happens to me and the police will be all over you."

Jones laughed. "Ah, Jeremy, Jeremy, you're so deluded. Sure, the cops might have a moment's doubt when you turn up dead. But with nothing but your cockamamie story to go on, it won't last. I mean, you're barely a step above homeless, living hand-to-mouth in this dump." He waved a hand at my building. "And who'll keep the search alive? Your parents are dead. You have no brothers or sisters. Not even a girlfriend. Nope, the police will forget all about you before the dirt settles over your dead body."

His words brought me up short as I stared at his shadow in disbelief. How did he know all that about me? None of that was on my application to work for Schmidt. That question, however, could wait. What couldn't wait was, how do I deal with him now?

I willed some quiet to my mind to focus on the possibilities. At the lab, it had seemed unlikely that reason would prevail, and it had gotten me nowhere. Now, calling on it seemed nothing short of laughable. That left action. Unfortunately, I had left my phone in the kitchen, and dashing back inside to retrieve it would just trap me there with Jones. Shouting for assistance also seemed wasted effort. Mine was a working–class neighborhood, and at this hour, nothing short of an 8.0 magnitude earthquake would wake them. I was on my own against Jones, either to overpower him or to find help to do so.

"Well, I guess your trip to the cops changed one thing," said Jones. "You aren't going to die from a gunshot. That might look a bit too suspicious. But driving your car off the river bluffs? Well now, that sounds like something a nutter like you would do. And a few extra bumps and bruises from my Louisville slugger here." He brandished a bat that I could barely make out in the moonlight. "Who would notice?"

Deciding on a course of action, I rubbed the sweat from my hands and slid forward in the chair. I leaned over slowly in the darkness, groping for the old brick that was my occasional front doorstop. As soon as my fingers brushed against it, I lofted it to my shoulder, the muscles in my legs and arm tensing in anticipation. I sprang out of the chair as my arm shot forward, hurdling the projectile toward Jones's head.

I missed.

I didn't miss Jones; I missed his head. By the time the brick reached him, it was chest high. And when it reached his torso, much to my surprise ... it passed right through. Jones spun around as the brick continued its flight and we watched as it smashed into the pavement, shattering into a cloud of dust and fragments under the streetlight. Then, he turned back to me, laughing.

"You're not the only one who can take advantage of quantum mechanics," he said. It was too dark for me to see, but Jones had to be wearing a second vest. And for his vest to be working, the rest of the Environmental Barrier equipment must be nearby, perhaps in his car. My eyes probed the darkness, but I saw nothing.

"What the hell does that mean?" I asked, not expecting a response so much as just wanting a few more seconds to think because, at the moment, my head was spinning. How could I overpower him when I couldn't even touch him? The image of me throwing a punch, only to see my momentum carry me right through him would have been hilarious, except that was exactly what I expected to happen if I tried.

But then, if I couldn't touch him, could he hurt me if my vest was on? On the chance that mine might work, I moved slowly, keeping my hand in the shadows as I flipped the power switch. I wanted whatever small advantage the element of surprise might give me.

I've heard that in the midst of a skirmish, veteran combatants experience a heightened sense of awareness as time slows, and every sight and sound is magnified. Unfortunately, that ability doesn't extend to those who are experienced only in the pushing, shouting, and shoving that's characteristic of all young men growing up. So, while I was busy with my sleight of hand, I completely missed what Jones was doing—taking aim and flinging his bat directly at my head. Without awareness of the danger, I didn't even flinch and the bat reached me almost perfectly centered on my nose. I would have been out for the count except my guess was right—my vest was working. I turned, as the bat passed through me and came to rest, innocently leaning up against the back of the chair where I had been sitting.

I blinked several times and swallowed hard, still getting my head around the situation. If it hadn't been clear enough before, it was now. Jones was prepared; I was not. And even though his plans might be as simple as wrestling me out of my vest and beating me to a pulp before running me off a cliff in my car, it was still more forethought than I could claim. Putting distance between us or finding a public spot gave me the best chance of leveling the field, and I bounded down my front steps, took a right, and headed down the street.

Glancing behind me, I took some comfort in the fact that Jones had taken a moment to retrieve his baseball bat. Then, I recalled why he had brought it in the first place and my relief disappeared.

During that glance, I also realized that Jones was slower than me. It made sense. He was probably 35 pounds heavier. But the additional bulk was not fat; it was all muscle. So, while I would be able to outrun him in a sprint, over the long haul, he'd catch me. I also knew that what was 'the long haul' in this context was not as far as I might hope. My recent history of doing as little as necessary to get by was working against me. I was out of shape. I vowed that if I survived the night, I'd return to my habit of jogging tomorrow. OK, maybe the day after, because I was going to need tomorrow for sleep.

I glanced back again and he was gaining already. The shock of that thought dumped another shot of adrenaline into my bloodstream, and I picked up the pace to match my racing heart. But I wouldn't be able to do that many more times; there was a limit to the body's emergency stores and mine would be depleted soon. I needed to increase the gap between us, but without relying solely on speed and endurance.

Maybe a little subterfuge?

Looking right and left, I felt a wave of relief as I spotted what I needed. Sprinting across the street, I barreled into a six-foot-high, wooden, privacy fence surrounding a backyard. I thought about slowing down, wondering if the Barrier technology in Jones's car would reach this far. But in the end, I decided it was better to hit the fence at full speed and knock myself out if the tech failed. That way, I wouldn't have to see what was coming. But the technology didn't fail me, as I found myself staring at a child's swing set and a barbeque grill.

Here, I was out of sight. Here, I could vary my path and Jones would have no way to know. He might guess my direction once, or even twice, but he'd never be able to find me if I kept zigging and zagging out of his sight.

In the first backyard, I went right. The next fenced yard was only 4 houses away, and this time, I went straight. Then, a left in the next, and then, another straight ahead. I was starting to feel a bit safer, which was fortunate, as my lungs were burning and my legs were starting to feel weak and rubbery. Gaining the sanctuary of another yard, I sat down on the chair of a patio set. If anyone woke up and turned on the backyard lights, I could just race through the fence and they'd chalk it up to a late-night, bad dream. But no lights came on, and no one appeared. That was until Jones showed up.

"What a nice place for a break, huh, Jeremy? Maybe I'll get me a set like this with the money in your pocket."

What the ...?

I sucked in a quick breath, my heart skipping a beat. How could he be so lucky? I raced off through the fence ahead, the three-minute break apparently all that I was to get.

As I continued down the street, I scanned the night sky, hoping to spot the telltale light of an open business. There, to the left, about two streets over was a glow much too intense for a street light. I took a meandering route to that spot via three more backyards, only to find a fenced parking lot ringed by a set of floodlights. The gleam of yellow metal from the fleet of school buses parked there was almost blinding.

I continued down the street. A block away, I spotted another glimmer and laid down another twisting trail through fenced yards. Here, I was treated to a couple of thousand watts shining on a billboard for running shoes. The ad seemed almost cruel in its irony. Where were the all-night gas stations and convenience stores when you needed them?

I hung my head as I trotted down the street, partially because of these disappointments, but mostly from fatigue. It was still dark, but it had to be getting close to morning. People would start getting up soon. Maybe someone would see us and call the police. Of course, it would be better if the police saw Jones chasing me. Otherwise, I'd have to claim that someone whose real name I didn't know was chasing me for a reason that I couldn't explain involving a crime that another department had declined to investigate. Yes, my story to the police would have the weight of fog on a summer's breeze.

But the positive from all these dead ends, if there was one, was that I had completed a long set of twists and dodges that I felt certain no one could follow. Gaining access to a final yard, I dropped to the ground beneath a tree. I gasped for air and tried to massage some feeling back into my legs. After about five minutes, I started to relax, thinking that I had finally lost Jones ... when I heard his voice. "Do you have any idea where you are?" I could just see his eyes, peering over the fence to my left.

I would have gasped, but I didn't have the breath. The renewed threat should have energized me, but my reserves were gone. The best I could do was to stagger to my feet and lumber through the fence to my right.

Again, I wondered how Jones was finding me so fast, but the pain in my legs and in my lungs was making it nearly impossible to concentrate on anything other than it. But a thought did come to me. Perhaps my tactic of using fenced yards was working against me. Maybe Jones had doubled back and gotten his car so he could drive around and check all the possibilities. It seemed like fenced yards were common but maybe tall, privacy fences weren't as numerous as I thought.

But whatever the flaw in my thinking was, I now found myself down to the last option—go pound on someone's door, hope they were a light sleeper, and beg them to call the police so I could deliver my far-fetched story. Even being thrown in jail for creating a public disturbance sounded better than facing Jones and his bat.

Choosing a house randomly, since I didn't know the style preferred by insomniacs, I raced up the front sidewalk. I stole a glance behind me and saw no one, which was good because I was desperate for a break. I raised both hands, intending to start pounding the instant I reached the door, and ... I went flying through it.

I collapsed to the floor, holding my head in my hands, trembling from the exertion and my inability to focus. Of course I went through the door. The vest was turned on.

I slowly rose to my feet, shuffled over to a chair, and took a seat. I felt very uncomfortable making myself at home but decided that after a few minutes' rest, I'd go back outside, turn off the vest, and knock. I just hoped that if someone found me here, they would understand my predicament. But understanding would be difficult for anyone. Even to me, what was happening seemed impossible.

Some of the house's facade had registered when I had run up the steps. It was a two-story Victorian, with a single, large front door on the right side, and a three-window bay on the left. The second floor repeated that pattern, except that there was a window in place of the door. A decorative cornice completed the look. As my heart rate returned to something more near normal and my breathing slowed, I looked around the room. It probably would have been considered the parlor, in the day. Now, it seemed to be used as an informal living area, with a mixture of comfortable-looking chairs and a couch, with some Victorian-era accent pieces—a fainting couch and a Victrola. I could personally attest to the fact that the chair I had selected was as comfortable as it looked.

As I relaxed further, I heard a faint tone coming from the vest. I had heard it before, almost every day at the lab. The vest was nearly out of power. Since my life might still depend on it working, I shut it down to conserve whatever was left in the battery.

With the hum of technology gone from my ears, I heard another sound. It was running water. But it didn't sound like a sink or a toilet. It was a rushing, splashing noise. Could it be a burst pipe? Maybe the owners had left on vacation and would be coming home to find a flooded basement. Having lived through that once when I was living on the Hill, I wished it on no one. I decided to take a peek.

Slowly and quietly, I crept to the back of the house. The sound was coming from a room just to the left of the kitchen. I figured it was most likely a butler's pantry, which had probably been modernized to become a mudroom or laundry area. I tried to stick my head through the door to take a look, only to crack my already sore forehead on the wood. Just moments ago, I had berated myself for forgetting the vest was on and now, I had forgotten it was off. I must be exhausted.

With the power off, I'd have to do this the old fashion way. I slowly turned the doorknob and pushed the door open, just as the splashing, gurgling sound stopped. And there, standing in front of me was a young woman, who had just stepped dripping wet from the shower. With a slender, athletic build, she appeared the flawless combination of firm and lithe, smooth and curved, in all the right places and in the perfect proportions. Her pale face and deep hazel eyes were framed by long, dark brown hair, which appeared almost black when wet. She was, in a word, beautiful.

I, on the other hand, was unnerved. How had I been so careless as to have stumbled upon her, invading her home and her privacy? While I had an almost endless supply of excuses born of desperation, none seemed to cover such a crass blunder. I didn't think she had seen me yet, but she soon would, as she dried her face with a towel. I wasn't going to wait to see her response, as I blurted, "Sorry, wrong house." I immediately stumbled back into the door jam in my haste to flee, saying "Sorry" a second time, not knowing if it was another apology to the woman for my indiscretion or one for the door. I spun around and fled from the bathroom, finding renewed energy in my embarrassment.

The woman screamed, then yelled, "You better run. I'm calling the police."

I switched the vest on, planning to escape via the front door. But in my humiliation, I had become disoriented and I was headed through the kitchen toward the back of the house. I didn't want to turn around and chance running into the woman again. So, I sprinted straight ahead through the wall, only to find that floor level inside the house was more than four feet above the ground in back. I hit the lawn hard but managed to roll with the impact and jump to my feet running. Obviously, I had to find another door to pound on.

The corner was only two houses away and when I reached it, I looked down the street to the right. There was Jones, just a half-block away, getting out of his car. He had been driving, spared from the grueling cross-country race I was running. I bent over, putting my hands on my knees and gasping for air, even though I had run less than 30 yards since fleeing the house. I could almost feel the last of my resolve drain from me. Perhaps I should just sit down and beg him to make it quick. It was tempting because whatever I did, he was there, always gaining, always running me to ground. Wasn't surrender sometimes the only option?

But then, maybe surrendering had become too easy for me. There was some truth, I knew, in Jones's words about my near homeless, hand-to-mouth life. And this surrender, if I did, would be my last. I couldn't do that. I needed to give it one more try.

By now, I was totally lost; nothing looked familiar. But if I continued along the street, there was an open area ahead on the left. It was something like a park but poorly tended.

The grass was long. I could see it waving in the moonlight. And beyond that, there was a dark line of trees. Perhaps I could find a hiding place there. Certainly, nothing else was working. I took off across the grassy area, knowing that Jones was only steps behind.

As I approached the tree line, a stolen glance behind made it clear I was not going to make it. Jones was only about 10 feet back. I had just decided it was time to turn and see if I could wrestle his vest off before he got mine when I tripped over something half-buried in the weeds. It was the remnants of a chain-link fence, probably crushed by kids using this field as a short cut to whatever lay beyond the trees.

Resting across what was left of the fence was a long, metal pole of the type that would have originally run along the top. But now, it formed a lever, with the smashed fence as the fulcrum. And when I stumbled over the fence, I had hit one end of the pole causing the other to fly skyward. Somehow, for the second time in two days, I had managed to hit Jones in the groin. He doubled over, using what I was certain was every bit of profanity he had ever learned to disparage me and my lineage.

I collapsed to my knees, panting as I tried to regain my breath, if not my energy. But even that took second seat to retrieving the pole that I now considered magic. When nothing else seemed to work, I had been able to use it to stop Jones.

Eventually, his vulgarity-laden tirade slowed and he stood upright. "Jeremy ol' boy, you're the luckiest SOB I've ever met. But you know this can't last. I'm thinking that was your last rabbit's foot."

"Not so quick," I said and poked the pole at his chest. But it passed right through as if it had made contact with nothing but thin air. "What the ...?" I gasped, taking a quick step back. Maybe it was the point of attack that made the difference, so I aimed lower. Again, I felt no resistance. The only effect was to make Jones angrier, as he glared at me, his face turning even darker. If it was some type of intermittent fault in the Barrier technology that was letting the pole hurt Jones one minute but not the next, it was starting to wear very thin and I cursed its unpredictability under my breath. Turning, I headed for the trees, still clutching the pole, just in case.

The break had helped me regain some momentum and the shot to Jones's southern regions had slowed him. But even so, he was holding his own, maybe thirty yards back now. As I entered the tree line, I started looking left and right, high and low, for any place of refuge. Where I wasn't looking, however, was straight ahead. The next thing I knew, I was falling face-first toward a moonlit patch of flat rock.

Of course, in these split seconds, I was still reacting like I would pre-Barrier technology. In other words, I braced for the impact. But it never came. What did come, however, was much worse. The flat rock was actually a shelf out over the Mississippi bluffs, and I had passed through unscathed ... for now.

There are places on the bluffs, of course, where you might fall 50 feet or more. But such places are rare. Mostly, you'd fall something between five and twenty feet and maybe twist an ankle or break an arm when you land. And then, you'd roll another 150 feet, hitting every tree and boulder until you came to rest, looking much like a mound of raw hamburger. It was not something I was looking forward to.

But as I passed through the rock ledge and into free fall, I could feel a tug on my arm. I was still clutching the pole, desperately. It was just instinct, I guess; it certainly wasn't a logical, reasoned decision. But as I gripped it, I could feel the pole holding me back, as if it was caught on something. And then, its motion stopped, and I swung back against the bluff face. I grabbed a root sticking out there, as the pole then broke free and fell to the ground below. I looked down. If I dropped from here, the fall would be only about another eight feet. Beyond that drop, however, I could see little that would stop me from tumbling downhill for another 20 yards.

Looking up, I could see the ledge above me, only about five feet away. There were other roots and limbs that I could use to make the climb. I was about to head up when Jones appeared. I pressed myself into a small crevice in the rock face below the shelf, trying to be as quiet and small as possible. In my state of exhaustion, I could feel my arms trembling. I tried to slow my breathing, hoping to make less noise, but I was so out of breath from the run, it was still coming in soft gasps.

Finally, I heard Jones mutter to himself, "Damn, that's a fall. Looks like the end of the line for ol' Jeremy." He turned to leave, probably to find a way down to confirm my demise.

When he was gone, I struggled to the top of the cliff and laid down on the mossy ground. Sometime in the last few seconds, my vest had either been damaged, or all of the power had been expended. It had been working when I passed through the rock shelf, but now, it was off, as the telltale vibration was gone. I hoped it just needed charging because I wasn't at all certain that I had seen the last of Jones.

5. My guide

After my narrow escape on the cliffs above the Mississippi, Jones seemed to disappear. I wasn't sure if he couldn't find me, or if he'd just had enough fun for one night. Whatever the reason, I wasn't complaining, because I was exhausted. I had no idea exactly how far I had run, but the 26.2 miles of a marathon couldn't be too far off.

Now that I was free of my tormenter, the effort and stresses of the last day came crashing down on me. Going home and sleeping in my own bed wasn't safe. Jones might be there already, waiting in the dark. And even if he wasn't and came by later, I'm certain it would be harder for him to wake me than it would be for him to finish me off in my sleep. But making decisions about any other arrangements for the remnants of the night was proving impossible; my mental fatigue matched my physical exhaustion. Finally, I stumbled on another small park—not much more than a triangle formed by three intersecting roads. Finding a relatively secluded spot away from any sidewalks, I settled in for a short nap, just as the first glow of dawn showed in the east.

When I awoke, the sun was already high in the sky. I got up, but only with great difficulty. Everything hurt—my arms, my legs, my feet, my hands, my knees. But it was my head that was the worst off. Just how hard had I hit that metal plate? It was still sore to the touch and was producing a throbbing pain at my temples.

As much as I had enjoyed my current accommodations, huddled under a layer of dry leaves I had scraped together before dozing off, I couldn't count on them for another night. The weather forecast on the car radio during the trip from the police station to the lab last night had mentioned rain and rapidly falling temperatures. But that was St. Louis in the fall. It could be 70 degrees and sunny one day, and drop to 30 with freezing rain that night. So, in forming my priorities for the day, finding temporary shelter came in only slightly behind cleaning up and getting something to eat. The energy from those three burritos had been expended within the first few hours of last night's jaunt and my legs and arms were shaky.

After wandering for a few minutes, I got my bearings and headed for another, more sizable park nearby. It was late enough in the year that the water supply to most of the outdoor restrooms would be shut off, but this park had a small, information office with facilities that were available year-round.

Looking in their mirror, it was worse than I thought. My forehead was covered in dried blood and there was a bruise the size of an egg. The rest of my face was streaked with dirt and covered with small scrapes and scratches. Likewise, my clothes were filthy and my jeans were ripped at the knee. Too bad Halloween was over; I already had the perfect zombie costume.

While most of my clothes were a complete loss, I hoped one piece of my attire had survived—the vest. When I checked it, I found that one seam had unraveled a bit and the cloth was caked with dirt, but overall, the electronics seemed to be undamaged. It really needed to be working, because I wasn't sure how to survive Jones without it.

As I washed, scrubbing my face, hands, and arms and trying to remove the worst of the grime from my clothes, a plan took shape in my mind. Going back to my apartment still seemed much too dangerous. There were too many places for Jones to hide. But retrieving my car from the street in front seemed a reasonable risk. After that, some new clothes, a decent meal, and a safe place to sleep would round out phase 1. I was hoping that phase 2 would come to me after my head stopped pounding and my stomach stopped growling.

On the walk back to my apartment, I noticed a restaurant with a drive-through window. The original order of the steps in phase 1 had been to get clothes before eating, but my head was not going to win this argument with my stomach. Using the drive-through would likely be less objectionable to the restaurants' patrons. Even so, the stares I received were nearly nonstop and uniformly unfriendly.

Now with the worst of my hunger pangs gone, I completed my hike and positioned myself across the street and half-way up the block from my apartment. I watched it for 15 minutes, seeing nothing. I suppose with training on how to do a stakeout, I would have stayed there for hours, maybe days. But the waiting was killing me, not to mention the itch and smell of my clothes. And my hunger was returning. It was time to make a move. I crept down the street, employing as much stealth as possible when there is little to hide behind other than the occasional parked car.

"Hey, Jeremy."

It was my neighbor, Larry McClure, from three houses up. He was one of the few on the block who knew me well enough to hail me on the street. And as was his custom, he did so at the top of his lungs. I wished he didn't know me so well.

Figuring that Larry wouldn't pick up on any hand signs to quiet down, I jogged over to him. But all the while, I kept glancing back at my apartment, expecting to see Jones burst out the front door with his guns blazing. Or maybe it would just be with his bat swinging. But nothing happened.

"What the heck happened to you?" Larry asked when he noticed my injuries and clothes.

"Just went canoeing with a friend and slipped in. I'm going to get cleaned up."

"Yeah, you might want to." His nose wrinkled as my odor reached him.

"So, we've crossed off skates, bicycles, Frisbees, and ladders," said Larry. "Guess we need to add canoes to the list."

Larry was keeping a list of all the things I should avoid because I'd had accidents while using them. He thought the list was hilarious; I thought it was annoying. And the Frisbee thing—it was a pure, freak accident. A 'what-can-I-say' shrug, hastened by my odor, sent him back into his house. And all through the conversation, there hadn't been so much as a curtain being parted or a door being cracked in my apartment.

Seeing little reason to be stealthy after Larry's shouted greeting, I walked over to my car, got in, started it, and drove away. A mirror check showed that there was no one following. I pulled over in a commercial area about half a mile away. Although not heavily traveled, there would be some foot traffic and the street lights were regularly spaced. Overall, it appeared to be a good place to leave my car, because in considering my choices, I had decided to go back for one more of my possessions—a 1999, 400cc Kawasaki motorcycle.

As my interest in work disappeared, I had sold a lot of my stuff to make ends meet. My TV went in a garage sale, because who needed one if you have streaming video? That decision came before I knew how slow my internet connection would be. A laptop went in an online sale, although I had another. The second one, of course, was for the video I couldn't stream. Even some of my old clothes went on the sales block, but I didn't clear enough to justify the effort of making a sign that said, 'your choice, 25 cents.'

But through it all, I had held onto my beloved bike ... because it really wasn't worth much. Why deprive myself of the simple pleasure of riding it for a few hundred dollars, at least until I had no other choice? So, I went back to my apartment and conducted a much shorter period of surveillance. Basically, I walked slowly down the street. Again, seeing no one, I retrieved my bike from the ramshackle garage in back. As the rain hadn't appeared yet, I left my car on the street in the commercial area, figuring I would get it later, when the need arose.

The rest of my errands were straightforward. A clothes store to buy a complete change came first—shirt, pants, socks, and underwear. Then, I went to a truck stop on I-55, heading south out of St. Louis that had showers. I cleaned up, changed, and put everything but my shoes and the vest into the trash. My hunger had returned, so before leaving I had one of the breakfasts that they served 24/7 and a half pot of coffee.

With my daily quota of calories reached, along with enough caffeine to keep me going for some time, my attention turned to problem-solving. The question was simple: how do I stay alive? It was the solution that was causing problems. But one thing I knew for certain—I was in over my head. From the beginning, it had never made sense that Jones was after me because of the money. Even if he wasn't the brightest bulb, risking death by lethal injection for $1,000 was insane. And that coupled with his dogged pursuit of me last night made it obvious. He wanted me dead for some other reason entirely.

Just what he wanted, however, was eluding me. It couldn't be the vest itself; he had one. But it also seemed impossible that it was unrelated; that would be too much of a coincidence. Rather, it seemed likely it was the plans for the device. It was at this point, however, where I got in over my head. What was this equipment that made going through solid objects possible? Much of the stuff in the lab was obviously a smokescreen and now sat unused in the community college's storeroom. And it was clearly small enough for Jones to haul it around in his car, letting us traverse every backyard in south St. Louis ... not to mention the occasional bathroom.

I winced again at the thought.

And then, there was the matter of Jones's comment that he too could use quantum mechanics. What the heck was that about?

And finally, how did Jones keep finding me so quickly? In my exhaustion during the chase, I decided he just went to yards with tall fences. But now, that seemed ridiculous.

There had to be dozens of them. He couldn't have picked the right one as quickly as he had. There was something else going on.

I knew that people could be tracked by the GPS in their phones. Even if the phones were off, supposedly, the GPS could be activated. Or, if you used your phone, someone could determine your position by triangulating the cell towers. Basically, if you had a cell phone, remaining off the grid might be nearly impossible.

Had Jones been tracking me that way? He just didn't seem the type. Accomplishing something like that would require some shrewdness, the right connections, and some discretion in their use. Jones was probably 0 for 3 on those requirements. But an old classmate in just the right job might be enough. Coming to this conclusion in the movies would have meant that the phone would be smashed by a hammer or ground to pieces under someone's foot. Due to my financial status, removing the back and taking out the battery seemed safe enough.

But addressing the other issues—what was the vest and did mine still work—would take a bit more effort.

An electronics store provided a small, commercial power supply of the type they'd used to charge the vest in the lab. From there, I went to a local branch of the St. Louis County Library. Spotting an available computer, I sat down, plugged in the power supply, and attached it to the vest. Using one of the bags from the store, I kept the dirty cloth out of sight. If anyone thought anything about a power cord going into a clothes bag, they didn't say anything.

Putting my concerns about the vest aside for now, because I had no other choice, I opened a browser on the computer and started a search. The easiest way to answer my questions about Jones was to find Dr. Johannes Schmidt. He would know where to find Jones, and then the police would quickly get to the bottom of this mess. But if Jones was trying to steal the plans for the technology, which was rapidly becoming my favored hypothesis, maybe he had already killed Schmidt and taken them. It was a cold thought, I admit, but if this was true, I'd be happy to work with the detectives investigating his death because that would keep me alive.

Detective Underwood said he had checked on Schmidt and had found no one that fit the description, but were his investigative skills any good? Maybe it was my ego talking, but I felt pretty confident in my computer searches. Typing the name into a search engine almost immediately returned 1,420,000 hits. Obviously, Underwood didn't know his job, or so I thought until I realized that most of these individuals didn't live anywhere near St. Louis, and many were dead, some for hundreds of years.

I needed to tighten the search parameters. But adding just about any restriction, such as 'St. Louis' or 'quantum mechanics,' returned no relevant results. There were Schmidt's in St. Louis, but with first names like William or Harold or Frederick. Or, there was a Johannes who was a physicist, but it was a Johannes Leibnitz. Detective Underwood probably knew what he was doing.

After failing to find any leads with the name, I looked up from the computer and scanned the room. Not much had changed in the half-hour or so I had been working, except for one recent arrival. And among the mothers chasing their kids, the occasional teenager probably cutting class, and a few men casually attired in jeans and sweatshirts, he was as inconspicuous as an elephant in an anthill. He was probably mid-30s, well-dressed and clean-shaven, with neatly combed, straight brown hair, and a square jaw. He immediately made me uneasy and I shifted in my seat, watching him closely. After several minutes, during which he showed interest in only the computer in front of him, I decided it was just nerves and went back to my task.

Focusing on the technology rather than the person was my next strategy. That, of course, had been Underwood's thought as well ... until I told him what the technology was. Then, his thought was that I was a nut job. But searching from the technology side of this question proved no easier. Any straightforward inquiry, like 'moving through solid objects' returned nothing but sci-fi books or academic explanations of why it was impossible. And using 'quantum mechanics' in the query led to overwhelming technical detail. I needed someone with a scientific background as a guide; I could be reading exactly how the Barrier technology worked and not realize it.

So, the next line of search became, who was doing this type of work ... whatever the phrase, 'this type of work' implied. St. Louis had its share of high-tech businesses—aerospace, with Boeing and the related companies, and medical research, with some nationally recognized hospitals, in particular. After entering a carefully crafted set of parameters and hitting return, the screen started to fill with cutting-edge research projects at local businesses. My mouth fell open, as the treasure trove of data continued to scroll across the screen.

And then, from the corner of my eye, I spotted Mr. Clean-Cut, standing up from his computer and heading my way. My heart was beating in my ears, as I grabbed the vest from the bag, threw it on, and was about to hit the power button.

Then, he passed me, embraced a striking young woman who had just entered the library, took the hand of a small child, and they all walked out together. Too much drama, too little sleep I decided.

After my vitals returned to something more like normal, I went back to the information on the computer screen. While it showed pockets of gee-whiz work that was mostly over my head, none seemed a good match, with the exception of Frontier Atomics. It wasn't that Frontier had a banner across their homepage that said, 'Home of Environmental Barrier Research,' but they had some cutting-edge projects that looked to be better prospects than anything else I had seen. At least, that was my best guess from their carefully worded press releases.

Then, I turned my attention to the universities. After a few more minutes, I had a set of three university research centers that seemed to be conducting possibly related work. Not bad. A couple of hours searching online produced a list of four suspect organizations.

The point of finding a 'guide' to the technology, however, was to avoid acting on my own uneducated guesses as to which organizations might be harnessing quantum mechanics to walk through walls. But there was a reason I wanted to start with my uneducated guesses. If one of these groups was the point of origin for the Barrier research, then they couldn't be the source for my guide. I would end up asking for help from the same people that wanted me dead. So, I tried to err on the side of including too many organizations in my 'no recruit' list.

My whole thought process, however, was making me wonder if I was becoming paranoid. Avoiding university research center X because someone there might want to kill me? But after a moment's reflection, I decided that paranoia was healthy for now, and I could move to riskier options if my first attempts failed.

So, where to find my technology guide? Ruling out Frontier and the three university centers helped a lot because after doing so, the selection was limited. And then, in checking the fifth page of hits on one of my searches, I found Diane Stapleton, MD.

Dr. Stapleton had been associated with one of the university research centers on my no-recruit list, as well as with a local research hospital. She had made a name for herself in nuclear medicine. I wasn't really clear what nuclear medicine and the Barrier technology might have in common, if anything, but she had to be in a better position to understand it than I. And the reason I did not disqualify her as a guide due to her previous associations was because she had left these organizations nearly a year and a half ago. Unless current events had been planned long ago, she would have no connection to Jones or Schmidt.

The online story about Dr. Stapleton was a human-interest piece, as she had made her way from "... the rarefied atmosphere of high-tech nuclear medicine to a small country practice." There was more in the article about why she had left, but I didn't read it; she sounded like the perfect guide to me. Jotting down the address to her office, I left to find her.

6. Old friends

parked across the lot from Dr. Stapleton's office, still reeling from what I had just learned. After leaving the library, I turned on the vest. To my great relief, I was greeted by its familiar hum. Everything was good—the sun was shining, the birds were singing, the vest was working. OK, actually, it was cold, dreary, and windy, but at least the vest was functioning. For my own amusement, I headed for a short iron fence surrounding a nearby parking lot, expecting to bang my shins as I tried to pass. I went right through.

Immediately, I dropped to the ground, my heart in my throat as I searched the streetscape for Jones. He and his car with the rest of the Barrier technology had to be nearby if I was walking through walls again. Shutting the vest down to conserve the battery—in case there was another chase in my immediate future—I watched and waited. But Jones was nowhere to be seen.

After hugging the earth and crawling between parked cars for 20 minutes in a failed attempt to spot him, I started wondering if using the Barrier technology had somehow changed me. So, leaving the vest turned off, I headed for the parking lot fence again. After stubbing my toe, I thought, nope, I'm still me. Still a little klutzy and solid as ever. After flipping the switch to the on position again, I passed through the fence with no resistance.

How can this be happening?

I turned the vest off, jumped on my bike, and raced about five miles from the library. Then, I jumped off the bike, turned the vest back on, and walked right through a short brick wall that surrounded an apartment complex there. I could see no way Jones could have gotten from the library, assuming he was there, to this spot as quickly as I. There was only one inescapable conclusion. All of the Barrier technology was contained in this one vest. I had everything in my hands ... whatever everything was.

After this revelation, which I was still trying to get my head around, I put the vest back into the clothes bag, strapped it securely to my bike, and rode to Dr. Stapleton's parking lot. There I sat, wondering what to do next.

The reason for my hesitation—other than still being dumbstruck by the power in this one small garment—was that the name on the office complex was not Stapleton. It said, Dr. Ralph Weathers. I wished I had read more of the online article. But what's the harm in walking into Dr. Weathers office and asking for Dr. Stapleton? I could always claim that the bump on my head was obviously in need of professional attention.

As I entered, the receptionist looked up and said, "I think you've come to the right place." I was surprised for a moment, thinking she meant I would find Stapleton here. But she was just talking about my bandaged and bruised body. "I saw you drive up on that motorcycle. Have an accident?"

She was about the age my mom would have been if she was alive, and she struck me as the motherly type, so I gave her my best, pathetic smile and said, "Yeah, you know how it is. Car drivers just don't see you. Had to dump it in a ditch alongside the road."

"Oh, my," she said, looking upset. "Anything broken?"

I had overplayed my hand a bit. "Oh, no. Just some scrapes and bruises, but I was hoping the doc could take a look at the bump on my head."

"Sure, Dr. Weathers has some time. Just fill out these forms." She handed me a clipboard with a few pages attached.

"OK, but I was hoping to see Dr. Stapleton."

The motherly look disappeared from the receptionist's face as she scowled at me. "Are you with the press?" she asked.

"The press?" I didn't have to act bewildered by her question, because I was. Could moving to a country practice, if you considered Robertsville the country, really be newsworthy a year and a half later? "No, I'm not from the press. I just heard her name and thought I'd ask to see her."

My denial, along with my rather puzzled expression must have gotten the best of the receptionist, as her glare softened. "Dr. Stapleton will be taking over the practice from Dr. Weathers in about six months, so I usually give him the walk-ins while she meets our regulars."

An offer to become a regular crossed my mind, but I worried that might make me look desperate, which wasn't far from accurate. The receptionist continued to frown at me, and just as I decided I wasn't going to pass muster, she said, "I guess it's OK. Fill out the papers and I'll get you in to see her."

I released the breath that I didn't realize I was holding and seated myself in a chair to complete the forms. A few minutes after I had finished them, the receptionist appeared at a door and said, "I'll take you back to an examination room now."

After the formalities of taking my weight, temperature, and blood pressure, I sat down in the exam room. Less than a minute later, the door opened and a stunningly attractive woman entered. She was dressed simply in tan pants and a white lab coat over a cream-colored blouse. Generally, when faced with a woman of such breathtaking beauty, I might have imagined the feminine body suggested by the soft curves in her attire. But in this case, imagination was unnecessary. That was because—I realized with growing panic—she was the same woman I had accidentally seen coming out of the shower this morning. My jaw dropped as my blood pressure shot through the roof.

"Jeremy Reynolds?" she read from the papers. Then, looking up, "Is there something wrong? You look a little ... upset."

"Sorry, I think I've made a ...," I started. But if I ran now, I'd have to find someone else to help me. Surely, if she recognized me, she'd be doing more than asking about my emotional state. She did seem somewhat perplexed, but nothing more than a slight confusion that I could tell. I decided to take a chance and hope for the best.

"Ah ... no, everything's OK. It's just .... I don't know. You look so familiar."

What am I thinking?

You look familiar because I saw you naked coming out of your shower this morning? Come on, Jeremy. You might not be the smoothest guy around beautiful women, but you can do better than this. Get it together.

"I'm sorry, Dr. Stapleton, but you do look familiar. But you probably get that all the time."

"Well, no, not that I've noticed," she replied casually. "But actually, so do you ... although I can't say from where." I felt like I was about to pass out from holding my breath when, thankfully, she moved on. "So, you're in to have me take a look at these cuts and contusions from a motorcycle accident?"

"Yeah .... Yes, the crash. It wasn't that bad."

"Well, maybe I should be the judge of that," she said, smiling. I grinned back, not able to control my somewhat-over-the-top reaction. Even though it hurt when she removed the bandage, I was glad when the exam got started. It gave me a chance to keep my mouth shut because there wasn't room for another foot in there.

"Looks like you've been keeping this cut pretty clean. No redness. The bump on your head looks painful. Have you been having any headaches, confusion, or dizziness?"

"Some headaches, at first, but they're pretty much gone," I replied. "No dizziness. No confusion ... well, no more than normal."

"I assume that's a joke," she said.

I nodded, my silly grin returning. But at least she recognized I was trying to be funny.

"Do you know if you lost consciousness when it happened?" Stapleton asked.

"No, I don't think so." Then, she checked my eyes and my reflexes.

"You rode your motorcycle here today?"

"Yeah, is that a problem?"

"Maybe not the best idea for a few days. If you have any dizziness or disorientation, have someone bring you back, OK?"

"Sure."

She started cleaning and applying a new bandage to my head. Everything was moving quickly. If I didn't get to the point soon, I'd be on my way to ... well, wherever I was going next, without ever finding out if she might be able to help.

"So, this must be quite a change from nuclear medicine," I said, giving her my best smile. It seemed like an innocuous, opening remark to me, but she recoiled like I had slapped her in the face.

"What did you say?" she demanded.

"Uh ...." I stammered, swallowing hard as my mouth went dry. "I just meant ... well, this must be a lot different from when you were involved in all that medical research."

"How do you know about that?" she asked, an edge to her voice. Then, as if she suddenly remembered some class lecture on dealing with the deceitful patient, she said in her most formal, doctor's voice, "I'm almost done here. Just keep the cut clean and change the bandages. If you start getting headaches or experience any type of disorientation, have someone take you to a hospital."

Her advice had changed from 'have someone bring you here' to 'have someone take you anywhere else.' Obviously, she was upset and anxious to see me leave ... and even more anxious to make certain I didn't return. Once again, I kicked myself for not reading more about her online.

I thought about the hundreds of television shows and movies I had seen where detectives always came up with a convincing cover story, on the fly, to obtain whatever access or information they needed. So, I figured I had to play to my strong suit. I'd go for sympathy because I was a pathetic liar.

"Dr. Stapleton, I haven't been entirely truthful with you."

I half expected her to ask me to leave, accompanied by a threat to call the police. But she didn't. Rather, she asked, "Did someone do this to you?" She knitted her brows in concern.

My eyes went wide with a possible opening that I hadn't foreseen. Claim abuse, get her pity, and then her help. But I couldn't. Nothing was worth being that dishonest, even if I could pull it off.

"No," I replied. "What gave you that idea?"

She paused, shaking her head slowly, perhaps wondering if she dared get more involved. "Well, I've never seen the bottom of a ditch as smooth and flat as whatever hit your head. There even seems to be some type of small tooling mark or maybe a welding seam that shows up in the bruise."

I drew back slightly, surprised she could read so much from the injury. "You're right ... of course. It wasn't a ditch. I ran into a large, flat metal plate."

"Well, the mark is faint but definite. You must have hit it pretty hard."

"It was an accident, just not one involving a motorcycle. But for me to understand how it happened, I have to ask about ... well, a field I know nothing about, but you may. What do you know about quantum mechanics?"

She laughed, covering her mouth with her hand. Then, as if she was embarrassed, she pressed her hand more firmly to her face, but her shoulders still shook for a moment. Finally, she said, "I'm sorry. That was terribly unprofessional. But after claiming you had no ill effects from hitting your head, you ask me about quantum mechanics?" She looked at me more closely and smiled. Her eyes seemed to twinkle. "I'm really sorry, but I know nothing about it. I'm a medical doctor."

"One with a background in nuclear medicine," I persisted.

That removed the smile from her face and she continued more firmly. "Why do you keep bringing that up? That's the past. And besides, nuclear medicine has nothing to do with quantum mechanics. I was studying the use of very small doses of radioactive materials for diagnostic tests in children. Quantum mechanics ... well, it's about states and behaviors of atoms and atomic particles. And in that sentence, I pretty much covered everything I know."

I dropped my head, looking at my hands in my lap, and sighed. "Oh, I thought they were more closely related than that."

"No, not really," her tone softening. "But what even makes you think you need a quantum mechanics expert anyway? It's not exactly the most common field."

"I'm not sure," I replied slowly. "It's just something that someone said."

Maybe it was time to cut my losses and leave Dr. Stapleton alone. I wasn't confident that I was getting anywhere, except building doubt in my mind about this approach. But still, she had to know a lot more about the science in the vest than I did. I had intended to take a class in physics my sophomore year in college, but my plans had changed and I ended up with absolutely no background in this area. Zero. Zilch. Nada.

I thought it was worth one more shot. "But as a doctor, you would have had classes in physics, right?"

"Yes, of course, but not the kind of theoretical and advanced coursework you're talking about. Look, if this isn't a medical problem—and I define that term very broadly— then I don't think I can help you."

"Could you just take a look at something. It won't take long, and it's right here in this bag."

"Stop!"

It was one of those no-nonsense, authoritative commands at a notch above a normal speaking volume that no one could ignore, like 'hands up,' or 'get your hand out of the cookie jar.' I froze. Then, someone tapped on the door of the examination room, it swung open a fraction, and the receptionist stuck her head in.

"Is everything all right, Dr. Stapleton?" she asked, a slight frown directed at me.

The doctor looked at me a second as if weighing her options. "Yes, Doris. I'll just be a few more minutes with Mr. Reynolds." When the receptionist was gone, Stapleton said, "I'm not sure what you have in there, but whether it's animal, vegetable, or mineral ...."

"It's electronics," I interrupted.

"Equally bad, and probably worse. This building is loaded with expensive, electronic equipment. I won't have you turning on whatever it is you have in there. And if this is something you have been using on yourself and it led to your injuries. Well, it needs to be destroyed. Or at least turned over to someone who can handle it with the care it deserves."

"Sorry, Dr. Stapleton, but you're getting the wrong idea," I pleaded. "It didn't hurt me. In fact, if I had been using it, I wouldn't have gotten hurt at all. And it's not habit-forming, or hallucinatory, or whatever, if that's what you're thinking."

"I'm thinking you're using something you don't understand and have no idea what it's doing to you."

That caused me to pause and I rubbed my forehead while considering her words. "I can't really disagree," I finally said. "But my objective isn't to continue to use it, but just ...." I struggled for the right words.

"Just what?" she asked.

"Just learn enough about it that I know who to give it to." Perhaps that wasn't exactly what I intended, but it was close. And it seemed a lot better than saying, 'just learn enough that I can find whoever is trying to kill me.' Because after that mystery was solved, I would return the vest to Schmidt.

Now, it was Dr. Stapleton who paused in thought. I could imagine the debate in her mind. Try to help this confused, complete stranger on a problem that is clearly not medical or be rational. I smiled, trying to look trustworthy, certain that bewilderment was already apparent on my face.

Finally, she said, "OK, so I take a look at these electronics and then, you hand it over to the authorities?"

"If that's what you recommend, yes. Your judgment is good enough for me."

Her eyes narrowed, so I continued before she had the opportunity to question me further. "So, where can I show it to you?"

That didn't sound quite right, even to my ears, so I quickly added. "Somewhere public would be good, as long as we can step away from the crowds for a moment. Something like the stacks in a public or university library would work perfectly." I could see myself, donning the vest and stepping through a wall of books as she gaped in amazement.

"I'm not too sure about that. I haven't been back in the stacks with a guy since college."

I'm certain it was an innocent comment, but again, the image of her coming out of the shower popped into my mind and I blushed. She looked shocked by my reaction and said, "I wasn't doing that!"

"What, you didn't kiss him?" I said, surprising myself with the comeback.

She gave me a mock exasperated look, as she shook her head. She did have a sense of humor.

"This is probably the worst decision I've ever made," Stapleton said. She stopped and stared at me as if she was still considering whether to just show me the door. Finally, she continued. "There's a place where you can show that thing to me. You know the mall down off Gavelton Road? Not so busy that you'd have a hard time finding a place for your demonstration, but public enough that you're either being truthful with me or you'll be headed to jail in handcuffs."

"Fair enough," I said. "So, shall we meet around 7:30 at the mall? Or is that too late with the long day you've had?"

"How about 6:00, outside the theaters?" she asked.

"It's a date." I winced as the words left my mouth, feeling my cheeks starting to warm. Somehow my fantasies had taken control of my tongue. "Not a date ... I mean ... just a time to meet."

"I'll see you then," she said with a slight smile playing across her lips, and she left the examination room.

Well, I had my shot at recruiting some help, and I was certain I was going to dazzle her.

7. Hanging at the mall

spotted Dr. Stapleton when she was still 20 yards away, walking down one of the wings of the mall toward the theaters. She'd changed after work, as she now wore faded jeans and a dark blue sweater, in deference to the cooler evening temperatures.

"You look great, Diane. I mean, Dr. Stapleton."

It just came out, as I felt my face turn red. I wasn't following the old adage, think twice before you speak. I wasn't even thinking once, and now I was really expecting a reminder that this meeting wasn't social; it was pity. Or worse yet, I'd get a slap in the face, never to see her again.

But in the few seconds it took for my misstep, Diane's expression went from surprised to amused. "Thank you … Jeremy. I guess first names are alright, away from the office. Just don't let Doris hear you call me that, or she'll be setting you straight about my title."

"Yeah, she did strike me as the protective type," I replied, feeling pleasure at gaining a first name basis. "And you really do look very nice."

She smiled, glancing down before she brought her eyes back to my face. "I thought I might as well be comfortable for your show and tell. I think they're working on some of the shops along that wing to the left. There should be some quiet spots there."

We started off down the hall.

"So, I've been thinking since we talked," she said. "I'm pretty sure you're not the inventor of these electronics you're about to show me."

I laughed. "Yeah, that would be a safe bet."

"And maybe I'm putting too much faith in my first impression, but I'm guessing you didn't steal it."

"No," I replied firmly. "Absolutely not. But it's a murky situation." I rubbed the back of my neck, wondering how much more I should say. While I couldn't be certain, knowing about the device seemed like it could put her in danger. But telling her my objectives seemed safe enough.

"Actually, I may be keeping this device from being stolen. I've been trying to find the person who built it because I think someone else is trying to nab it." I glanced at her, but her eyes were forward as we continued to stroll down the hall.

"And you can't find him? The inventor, I mean."

"No, I can't. And neither can the police."

"Then, you've been to the police about this?" she asked. I thought I heard a bit of relief in her tone.

"I have. They tried to help, but no luck."

"And now you're hoping with my past, I might know something that helps you find him?"

"Yeah, basically. I guess there's also the chance that the inventor doesn't want to be found. It's a significant technology—really, spectacular, so maybe he is trying to keep it and himself out of the public eye. That would be possible, wouldn't it?" I asked.

"Sure. Until it's patented, most inventors would be secretive, maybe even to the point of being paranoid. No one wants to lose years of work to someone who grabs the plans and gets to the Patent Office before they do. Is that what you think is going on?"

"Maybe. Like I said, the inventor seems to have dropped from sight. But even earlier, he was doing a lot of things that would make it difficult to trace him, like creating a business that doesn't exist."

"That is a bit strange," she said slowly.

I glanced over again, and although she was still looking forward, I could see she was biting her lower lip. I wanted to say more, but I had already involved her more than I had planned. To get into specifics, like names and places—that could only lead to problems. If something happened to me and she was to act on anything I had told her, even by going to the police, she might end up in the same position as I now found myself.

"This looks good," I said, pointing to a shop in mid-renovation. One side was blocked off with yellow, construction tape, but the other wall was exposed. By standing at the end of that partially completed wall, Diane would be able to see me enter it on one side and emerge on the other.

"Ah, yes, complete with the low-level lighting to hide the sleight of hand," she joked.

"Well, I could ask them to bring up the lights, but trust me, there'll be no trickery. Stay right here," I said, as I stepped to the right side of the wall and donned the vest. I switched on the power and started to step forward, but then, stopped. "Don't you want to do a drum roll or something?"

"Come on, Jeremy. You're …."

But before she could finish, I stepped through the wall and appeared on the other side. Diane gasped, her hand flying to her mouth. She just stood there, eyes blinking. It seemed like a full minute. Finally, she asked, "How did you do that?"

"That's what I brought you along to answer. How does this vest work?"

"It doesn't," she said, still staring at the wall in disbelief. "It can't. It's impossible. A solid object can't pass through another solid object."

"Trust me, I've had more than my fair share of me not passing through solid objects." I pointed at the bruise on my forehead. "But I've also had hundreds of recent experiences where I've done exactly that."

"You know what an atom is, right?" she asked.

"Well, yeah, the basics, from high school. A nucleus with protons and neutrons, surrounded by electrons in orbit."

"Yeah, exactly. What is it that you do again? I forgot if I saw it on your form."

"Before I started walking through walls, I was an accountant," I replied. "But I'm sort of between accounting jobs. So, mostly I've been doing temp work recently, like the research project with this vest." This was about the most positive way I could think of to describe my mostly aimless approach to life over the last two years. Well, at least without claiming that I was trying to find myself.

"You've got the basics of an atom down," said Diane. "And the part of those basics that makes what just happened impossible is that one atom can't pass another closer than the outside orbit of electrons. If you tried to push two atoms by each other closer than that, the electrons couldn't share the same quantum state and would repulse each other. It can't be done."

"I knew you knew more about quantum mechanics than you admitted." I grinned at her, but she just frowned in return, arms crossed over her chest. "OK, it can't be done. But if it was done, how would it happen?" I asked.

I could tell Diane was wrestling with an almost irresistible urge to say, it can't happen, let's move on to explanations based on something more reasonable like a magician's tricks. But the flickering changes in her expression suggested she was working on the problem against her better judgment.

Finally, she said, "I'm not going to be able to come up with the how. If atoms are passing closer than the width of their outer electron field, it's way, way over my head. Way over. But I can make some wild speculation about what happened."

"Your wild speculation's better than anything I've got," I said. "So, what happened?"

"Whoever built this device found a way for atoms to share their empty space."

"I don't get that," I said. "Atoms have empty space?"

"Yeah, lots of it. Something like 99.99% of an atom is empty. Every college physics professor has his or her favorite analogy, but the one I liked the best was, if the nucleus was the size of a golf ball, the first electron orbit would be about a half mile away. That's how much empty space there is."

"Wow. Sounds like a lot of room to work with."

"Yeah, well having space and making use of it are two different things entirely." During most of this description, Diane had continued to stare at the wall I had transited. But with the break in the conversation, her eyebrows furrowed as she looked at me. "So, what's it like to go through something solid?"

I smiled at her because I had felt that same curiosity for a long time. "Like nothing's there. When I first started on the project, it felt sort of like walking through water. There was some resistance and you had to push through. But they kept working on it until now, I don't feel anything. The only way you know you are passing through something is that everything becomes a blurry gray for a moment, and then you come out. Want to give it a try?"

She paused, looking past me at the wall and chewing on the inside of her lip again. In the end, she said, "Maybe later."

"Who's your brainy friend, Jeremy ol' boy?" came Thomas Jones's voice from behind us. "I heard what she said about atoms. No dummy that one."

I spun around to face him. He had brought company, as another man, even brawnier than Jones stood beside him. His white T-shirt stood in stark contrast to Jones's black one. Both were carrying ball bats. I scanned the area for the police. There were none in sight. It was too early for the mall cops to be on duty. I glared at the men. My hands clenched into fists, preparing for the next iteration of this nightmare.

Spitting the words, I said, "Well if it isn't Thomas Jones. How'd you find me?" But before I had even finished the question, I knew—he had to be tracking the vest. The possibilities had been rolling around in my mind, and this was the only one that fit the facts. Jones, however, had a different answer.

"Where else would you be besides showing off for some girl at the mall?" he cracked. "What's your name, hon?" his tone syrupy sweet.

Diane started to step forward when I growled, "Leave her out of this. She has nothing to do with it."

"Too late for that, Jeremy. With all the talk of atoms, I'm betting you gave her a demonstration. And we told you what would happen if you did that."

"I'd be arrested on charges of industrial espionage?" I said, still glaring at him. "I didn't know you worked for the FBI?"

Jones turned red, the muscles in his jaw working. "We'll see how funny you are with a couple of broken legs."

Only if you can catch me.

I grabbed Diane's hand. For a split second, she pulled back, but seeing the pleading look in my eyes, she relented. Then together, we dashed back through the wall. Diane screamed, and I looked at her to make sure it was just surprise and not pain. The wide-eyed look on her face told me all I needed to know.

Jones was wearing his vest, too, so he came directly for us. But his buddy, Muscles, evidently didn't have one, and he was detouring around the end of the wall. So, to keep the odds at two of us to one of them, I pulled Diane through the second wall of the shop, construction tape and all.

There was no scream from Diane this time, but she did manage to shout, "Can we use the doors? I'm getting whiplash from flinching."

"I'd like to say you get used to it, but you don't," I yelled in return as we continued our escape. "At least, not for a while."

When we emerged from the wall, we turned right down a hall, heading for one of the mall's exits. As part of the construction area, it was quiet here, and I saw no one nearby. I suppose Diane expected me to turn the vest off, as her free hand reached for the door handle as we raced toward the exit. Or maybe it was just habit. But in any case, we hit the door at full speed and passed right through it to the parking lot. All I heard from Diane this time was, "Damn." I knew the feeling.

Like the wing we had just left, the parking lot was nearly empty with just a few cars scattered here and there under pools of light. We turned right again, and I immediately saw the error in my decision. It wasn't as if I was trying to lead us into situations where the vest was the only solution, but we were headed into an area that had been fenced off to hold some of the construction materials.

I glanced back and just like the previous evening, Jones was gaining ground, slowly but surely. In the process of stealing that glimpse, I must have swerved a bit, but it was enough that I felt Diane's hand slipping from mine. I didn't think that physical contact was necessary for the vest to work, but I knew that if we were too far apart, she would slam into one of these fences or walls. After all, once I went through a wall, it wasn't like it stayed open forever.

I looked at Diane, shouting, "Keep up." Then, I released my grip for a second, wiped my sweaty hand on my shirt, grabbed hers firmly, and pulled her abreast as we hit the fence. No problems. No comments this time either as we were both too winded to say anything.

I took another right and headed back into the mall, hoping that maybe there would be a crowd. If nothing else, we could catch our breath in the safety of numbers. But business at this site had seen a serious decline over the last few years, and the only people I saw when we entered was an elderly couple going into a shop some 20 yards away.

I didn't need to look back and check on Jones anymore. By now, I could hear his footsteps behind us. He was close, very close. I tightened my grip again, hopefully alerting Diane that I was about to make an extreme maneuver. I planted my foot, planning to make a sharp right turn into a hallway. As big as Jones was, I didn't think he could be that agile and figured the sudden change in direction would make him break stride. That should allow us to gain some much-needed space. Our momentum, however, was too much, and instead of making the full turn, we veered through one of the walls on the side of the hall.

We found ourselves in a storage area with racks of clothes. We had slowed a little, so I tried a foot-plant-turn again, and it worked better. Now, we were headed back in almost the same direction as we had come, except we were a couple of rows of clothes over. We slowed and I put a finger to my lips in a sign for quiet. Sure enough, in a moment, we heard Jones dash by us off to our left. We continued forward and soon emerged not far from where we had entered the storage area.

"What's going on?" Diane asked in a hushed but urgent tone, as she stared at me.

"I'm really sorry, and I'll explain as soon as we're safe. But that trick won't fool Jones for long. We have to get out of here."

I grabbed for her hand, but she withdrew it. She crossed her arms over her chest. Her face was flushed. I didn't think all the color was from running. I closed my eyes for an instant, cursing the misjudgment that had put Diane in this position. Desperately, I searched for the right words to convince her.

"Diane, I'm really, really sorry, but you can't stay here. Jones will kill us. Let me try to get us out of here, and then you can hand me over to the police—or whatever you want to do. But please, I can't leave you here."

There was another moment of hesitation and then, she relented, holding out her hand. I grabbed it and we raced down the hall. It split into a V, and I opted for the left leg, only to find Jones's musclebound friend waiting for us there. He had an evil grin plastered on his face as he raised his bat and came straight for us.

We must have been at one end of the construction area because this part of the hall was blocked off by a velvet rope—the type you might see at a movie theater strung between metal stands that were about three feet tall. Getting beyond the rope, of course, didn't require a vest as Muscles simply unhooked it, grabbed one of the stands, and slung it at us. He missed, so I picked it up, intending to throw it back. A hit was too much to hope for, but that was exactly what I needed.

But on the backswing, the base to the stand came flying off just as Jones was rounding the corner of the V. It hit him in the side of the head, and he went down hard.

How the heck is this happening?

I stared at him, dumbstruck. Again, a common object, like the metal pole, had hit solid flesh and bone. I filed the fact away in my mind because there was no time to consider it now. Jones was stunned, making this the best opportunity for escape that we were likely to get.

Running from the construction area, we were soon back in familiar territory. That fact was important because now I knew where my motorcycle was. It was just past a shop that was straight ahead. Just then, Jones and Muscles appeared after rounding a corner about 25 yards down the hall.

"I've got a plan, but you need to trust me." I pleaded to her with my eyes, both my hands holding hers. Too much hesitation now would be fatal.

There was a moment of doubt on her face, but it quickly disappeared to be replaced by determination, as she said, "OK. Let's do it."

I grabbed her hand. We turned and ran through the back wall of the shop directly ahead. And just as I had thought, there was my bike. I tossed her the spare helmet, put mine on, and soon, we were flying down the pavement going north. Within moments, I could see Jones and his friend in my rearview mirror. They were both getting in their cars to pursue us.

In its day, I would have put my money on my 400cc Kawasaki, but its day had been in 1999. It still had good acceleration and decent top-end speed, but it would never beat the cars I saw behind us in a straight-line chase. But then, I had no intention of going straight. Or at least, not for long.

About 100 yards north of the mall, I turned right on Billingsley Road. It was clearly marked with a 'Road Closed' sign. I paid it no heed. And if Muscles and Jones saw it, they did likewise.

After about 50 yards down Billingsley, I glanced back and it was clear that Jones's friend had the faster car or the heavier foot. He was closing the gap quickly. It was at that point that we passed the second 'Road Closed' sign. Muscles didn't let up on the gas. If anything, he accelerated, so I did the same, coaxing every bit of speed I could manage from the aging engine. Soon, we passed the last warning, 'Road Closed.' The effect on Muscles was no different than before, and he seemed to find another millimeter of play in the gas pedal. Diane had also seen the signs and did react, but I gave her credit. All she yelled above the roar of the engine was, "I hope you know what you're doing."

So do I.

The concrete roadblock appeared ahead. At the speed we were traveling, it was a blur. I doubted I could stop if I wanted to. I could feel Diane's hands digging into my chest as she clung on with all her strength. I glanced in the mirror. The trailing car looked only a few feet away, gaining rapidly. And then, the barricade was a blur in the rearview mirror. We had passed through unharmed.

Muscles, however, must not have understood the whole thing about electrons not sharing quantum states and repulsing each other as he slammed into the roadblock at what had to be at least 120 miles per hour. There was a split second of brilliant light and an explosion so loud that it eclipsed the roar of the motorcycle's engine. Diane screamed and the road plunged back into darkness.

8. Spies like us

When we pulled off the road several miles from the mall, Diane took off the helmet, flung it to the ground, and dismounted the bike. "Why'd he do that?" she screamed. "Why? Why?"

I got off the bike and removed my helmet. I had turned off the vest soon after passing the roadblock. I was almost certain now; it had been leading Jones right to me.

"I don't know, but he probably thought the same thing as everyone else. That what we had done was a trick, and if we could do it, so could he." I tried to speak calmly, soothingly, but it was difficult as my heart was still pounding.

"That was horrible," she cried, putting her face in her hands. Then, looking up at me, she said, "When I knew it was coming, I couldn't look back. But I swear, I felt the heat from the explosion when he hit."

Diane's whole body was trembling, her face, ashen. I stepped forward, intending to put my arms around her and try to comfort her.

"Stay back," she shouted, holding a hand out in front of her. "I need some space."

She wrapped her arms around her shoulders and started pacing back and forth alongside the road. "I can't believe what's happened. Being chased through the mall by men who want to kill us? Having my atoms smashed through walls and fences? I admit. I was curious about that."

She stopped pacing, looking down at the gravel alongside the road for a moment. She started walking back and forth again. "But I wanted to take it slow. I didn't want to go running headlong into walls without warning. And then, flying down that road on your motorcycle and through that roadblock. And the horrible crash. I'm surprised I'm not throwing up."

My shoulders slumped as my resolve seemed to drain out on the side of the road. I felt terrible, having put her through this ordeal. "I never expected anything like this to happen. I'm really sorry. But after they showed up, I just couldn't see any other way to escape."

She stopped and looked at me, her eyes moist with emotion. "I hate to ask, but did you know we could just drive through that barricade?" Her voice trembled as she spoke.

I hung my head, unable to look her in the eye. "I was pretty sure."

She didn't say anything. I looked up. She was still trembling, standing on the side of the road, a hand over her mouth.

"I had driven the bike through one before—at a park not far from my apartment," I said. "But that time, it was just me. I wasn't positive that both of us would make it through." She deserved honesty.

Diane started pacing again, wrapping her arms back around her shoulders and looking at the ground. When she stopped and looked up, she spoke softly, "OK, I can see that you've stumbled onto something … well, possibly, world-changing … both in its potential for good and for bad. And with that kind of power, I can see why Jones and his friend want it and would kill for it. I guess I also see that we were dead if we hadn't gotten away. I just hope I'm not around when you guess wrong about something like that roadblock."

She shuddered slightly. Then, she stared directly at me, her hands quiet at her sides, her voice rising. "But that's about all I understand. You need to tell me exactly what's going on. Everything. And then, we're going to the police before anyone else gets killed."

"Of course," I said. After putting her life in danger, she had the right to know it all. And after that, if she thought the police was the best solution, we'd be on the same page; I shared that opinion. In my mind, it was just a question of whether we could get them to believe us or not. "There's a restaurant nearby where we can talk."

We drove there and entered. It was nearly empty. I asked for a booth near the back, we ordered a couple of drinks, and over the next hour, I told her everything, with one exception. I didn't mention exactly whose home I had stumbled into. I felt bad about not coming clean, as I had promised myself, but it seemed a detail better left unsaid, at least for now. Things seemed strange enough without mentioning this one-in-three-million chance meeting.

When I finished, I looked directly into Diane's eyes, took a deep breath, and placed my hands on the table in front of me. "Diane, I can't apologize enough for what I have done to you. I've gotten you involved in something dangerous and I never meant to. I really thought I had taken every precaution. We were meeting in a place only the two of us had discussed. And after we made plans, I stayed away from any place where Jones might see me—my apartment, the lab, even the police station. I stopped carrying my phone, thinking that maybe he was finding me that way."

She gave me a tired, sad smile, but at least it was a smile. "I'd be lying if I said I was happy about what's happened. Well, I guess it's been nice getting to know you, but over dinner and a movie would have been better."

I returned her smile, unsure why she didn't rue the moment I had walked in her office, but finding relief in the fact that she didn't. "But if what you've told me over the last hour or so is true—and I believe you're being straight with me—then, you accidentally got involved. And now I'm in it too."

"Unfortunately, I think you're right," I said. "I don't know why Jones wants to get rid of anyone who knows about the vest, but he does."

Our waitress wandered over, checking to see if we needed refills. When she left, I glanced back at Diane. She was still looking at me, the same tired smile in place.

"I don't see any reason why you need to go to the police with me," I said, although it wasn't the truth. With someone with her background and credentials standing beside me, the police would have a much harder time dismissing my concerns as the babblings of a down-on-his-luck, slightly concussed man. But I couldn't ask her to help fix a problem of my making. "I'll handle it."

Her smile grew both wider and sadder. "Thanks, that's sweet, Jeremy, but no. Unless you're going to ignore the fact I was at the mall, the police will want to talk to me anyway."

"Are you sure? Jones is a psycho. And I can forget to mention you. The police already think I lost half my marbles with the first encounter with the road plate."

She laughed softly. "All the more reason I should be there. Once we get the police on the case and Jones's picture on the news, he'll back off and leave us alone."

I took a deep breath, wondering if I should try to talk her out of it. But something about the look in her eye told me it would be wasted breath. "OK. Detective Underwood will have a much harder time ignoring it with two of us stating that we were attacked by Jones."

"Good. Then, that's settled," she said simply. "Do you want to borrow my phone to call him now and see when we can meet?"

"Sure," I replied. I dialed his number from memory, and after listening for a moment, I put my hand to the mouthpiece and said to Diane, "It's going to his voicemail." Then, back to the phone, "Hello, Detective Underwood. This is Jeremy Reynolds. Unfortunately, I've had another run-in with Tom Jones at the mall on Gavelton Road, and by now, you've probably heard about the crash nearby. The two are related. And this time, I have a witness. We'll both come by the department, first thing tomorrow morning."

"I feel better," said Diane when I hung up. "But it's still tough with the thought of that car smashing into the concrete wall running around in my head." She hugged herself again as if she was trying to contain a shudder.

"By the way, you said you told Detective Underwood about walking through the road plate, but he didn't believe you. Are you going to give him a demonstration of the vest tomorrow?"

It was a good question, and I rubbed my chin for a moment in thought. Finally, I said, "I don't think so. If he knows about the vest, he'll have to take it as evidence and that won't help them catch Jones. But mostly, I don't want to be without the vest as long as Jones is out there and has one of his own. It should only be a matter of a day or two and then, this contraption can go back to its rightful owner. What do you think?"

Diane nodded slowly. "I agree. So, shall we pay for these drinks and get out of here. Or do you just want to turn on the vest and we can sneak out through the back wall?" she asked, a conspiratorial smile on her lips.

"I don't think we should do that," I replied.

Before I could explain, she said, "Come on, Jeremy. I was kidding."

"Yeah, I know. I just meant I'm not certain we should be turning it on at all. Earlier, I suspected that Jones was tracking my phone, but I didn't bring it today. And this morning when he was chasing me all around your neighborhood, he always seemed to find me a lot faster than I expected. It was as if he knew where I was. So, the minute he showed up at the mall, I decided he must be tracking the vest."

Diane laughed. "That was the first thing you thought when you saw him?"

The incredulous look on her face made me laugh too. "OK, maybe not the first thing, but right after the surprise and the anger and all of the four-letter words, that was my first thought."

"And all I could think when I saw the bats was, why couldn't I live in a town where badminton was the favorite sport?" Suddenly, her mood turned serious as she said, "Let me take a look at that vest." I handed over the ever-present clothes bag and she took the vest out. "It's a good thing that what's inside is valuable because the cloth is ruined."

Then, she found a seam that was starting to open and pulled the thread. I gasped when the electronics spilled out on the table, but she seemed completely indifferent.

Our waitress took that moment to check on us again. "Anything else I can get you folks?" She glanced down at the pile of electronics and did a double-take. I thought about asking for some pliers and a soldering iron, but said, "Just the check, please." She shrugged and moved away to get it.

If I was surprised by Diane's direct attempts to unravel the mysteries of the vest, pun intended, then I was astounded when she pointed to one small box and said, "Here's the problem."

"What is it?" I asked, frowning as I stared at the component she had indicated.

"A GPS tracker."

"How do you know that?" I asked, rubbing the back of my neck.

"The whole, country doctor thing. It's just a cover. I'm actually a spy for the CIA," she said, completely deadpan. I chuckled, rolling my eyes. Her delivery was too flat to be anything but a ruse.

"Oh, and it also says GPS, right here on the side of the box," Diane said, holding it up for me to see. She took out her phone again, opened a browser, and searched on the model number. "Not even a particularly high-tech one either. It's $50 online. It lists uses like safety equipment for hikers or to put on delivery trucks."

"Yeah, well it kept me running all over south city," I said.

Diane pulled the device from its plug and laid it on the floor. "You want to stomp it or shall I."

"How about we give it to Underwood?" I asked, picking it back up. "Maybe Jones will come to him."

"Ah, tricky. I like it."

She smiled and in spite of all the stress of the situation, I couldn't help but think how dazzling it was when she did. I wondered, why when I met such an amazing woman would I have to have a half-crazed killer on my tail? I sat there, mindlessly fiddling with the tracker until Diane spoke up.

"Jeremy, are you still with me? Stocking up on tidbits you can mull over during the next life or death chase?"

I laughed. 'Stocking up on thoughts about you' would have been the truthful response, but I had no reason to believe she felt anything more positive toward me than indifference mixed with determination to see this problem solved. "I was just thinking about how long it's going to take me to sew that vest back together. I'm a real whiz putting buttons back on my shirt, so I figure it'll only take me about ... a week."

She laughed, unsettling me again with her smile. "You're not going to use that dirty fabric, are you? I'll sew you a new one."

"You can do that?"

"Yeah, of course. All us doctors can sew," she said laughing. "I'll just use the same stitches I use when closing after an appendectomy."

"Thanks," I said. "That should keep all the electronic guts in."

Diane groaned, rolling her eyes for effect. "Ouch, that was bad."

"Yeah, sorry. Sometimes I can't resist. So, when do you think you'll be done?"

Diane glanced at her watch, then paused a moment in thought. "You must be exhausted after the two days you've had and little sleep last night. And since you can't go back to your apartment, you want to crash on my couch tonight? I'll have a new vest by tomorrow morning and then, we'll both go see Underwood."

"Are you sure that's OK? I don't want to be a bother."

She gave me an 'are you kidding' look as if I could possibly be more trouble to her than I had already been. "Truthfully, I'll sleep better knowing you're downstairs. So, OK? My couch for the night?"

Over the course of the afternoon and evening, I had expected everything from being slapped in the face to being turned over to the police. But her simple act of compassion now took me completely by surprise and a wave of gratitude washed over me. I smiled and nodded at her, saying, "That would be great."

We paid, went out to the parking lot, and climbed back on the motorcycle.

"We can swing by the mall tomorrow for my car if it's OK with you," said Diane. "Right now, I'd just like to go home, get sewing, and then, get some sleep."

"Sure. Be easier to spot someone hanging around in the daytime anyway." I took off for her home. After a couple of miles, she tapped me on the shoulder and said into my ear, "Pull over for a minute." So, I found a spot near a street lamp, stopped, and we dismounted.

"I was just wondering," she said after removing her helmet, "how do you know the way to my house?"

As quickly as my spirits had soared when she had offered me shelter for the night, they plummeted with her question. I looked down. A car drove by, honking its horn as if we were invading its space, giving me a chance to study the loose gravel alongside the road while I searched for the best excuse for my earlier behavior. I thought about making something up, saying I figured her home was somewhere near her office, which it was. But part of correcting my blunder was owning up to everything I had done.

"I've been there," I said finally. I couldn't look at her, dreading the contempt I expected to find on her face.

"Very early this morning, perhaps?" But the disdainful tone I expected to hear was missing. I looked up, but the light was behind her, leaving her face in shadow. All I could see was her silhouette, as she loosely cradled the helmet in both hands in front of her.

Finally, I cautiously ventured, "I'm really sorry it happened. It was totally by chance when I was trying to get away from Jones. I told you about how I was trying to throw him off my trail." I was still rearranging some gravel with my toe, unable to stand still.

"You did, but you never said that my bathroom became part of that ploy." This time, there was no mistaking her tone. She wasn't angry; it was something else. Perhaps teasing? Perhaps some amusement at my discomfort?

I tested the waters. "You don't seem that upset by what happened."

"Oh, don't get me wrong, Mr. Jeremy Reynolds," she started. Now sure this was a mock dressing-down, I actually smiled at the way she used my full name; I quickly hid it behind my hand.

"I'm plenty mad at you," she said when she continued. "You nearly scared the daylights out of me." All I could think was that she needed a lot more practice at scolding someone if this was the best she could do.

She continued in a more even tone. "Seriously, I was startled, but by the time I got the water out of my eyes, you were gone. I hardly had time to get scared. But the way you disappeared without a sound? Well, that spooked me big time. I walked around my place for an hour, pepper spray in hand, checking doors and windows. I guess I can call the security company tomorrow, tell them I want to cancel my appointment. I'm certain they can't protect me from the vest."

"I'm sorry I didn't tell you before," I said apologizing again but then, I had a lot to apologize for. "So, you're not mad that I saw you ... you know ...."

"Nude?" she said since I seemed to be having trouble with the word. Another car passed, revealing the wry smile on her face in the headlights. "You're right. I do have a score to settle. Next time in the office, I'll need to do a full physical. And I'm really, really thorough."

I grinned, the tension in the situation now fully gone.

"So, is there anything else you haven't told me?" Diane asked. I started to respond, but before I could, she put a finger on my lips. It was a simple act, but I shivered with her touch. "You may want to think about this carefully," she said.

"I took five dollars from my mom's purse when I was seven." Diane just shook her head in feigned exasperation.

"How did you know that it was me, this morning, in your bathroom?"

"I didn't—well, not for sure anyway," she admitted. "But at the office, you said something about me having a long day. You might have guessed that, but actually, you knew. And a few minutes ago, at the restaurant, you said something about Jones chasing you around my neighborhood. The only way you'd know that was if you knew where I lived."

"You missed your calling. That was a shrewd piece of detective work."

She paused for a moment, then said, "You know, when I thought about it ... before I asked you to pull over. It had to be one of two things. Either you spent years and tons of money having the vest researched, then staged an elaborate save-the-damsel-in-distress play for my benefit that ended in someone's death, all to get a half-second glimpse of me coming out of the shower. That didn't seem very likely."

I chuckled. "Yeah, perhaps a bit over the top."

"Or," Diane continued, "it's been an eerily strange set of circumstances that led to us bumping into each other twice in one day."

"I can't argue with that."

We climbed back on the motorcycle. As we continued to her house, I swear she sat a little closer on the seat, held me a little more tightly around the waist. Then, she laid her head against my back. It felt good to have an ally against Jones and I started wondering.

Could it be more?

9. Last words

The next morning came quickly. I was just sitting up on the edge of Diane's couch, yawning and rubbing the sleep from my eyes when she padded downstairs in her bare feet, her brown hair falling loosely around her shoulders. It wasn't right that someone should look that good in the morning. It was just a pair of gym shorts and a Mizzou T-shirt, but in my mind, she couldn't have looked better in the most expensive negligee.

"What time is it?" I mumbled.

"About 8:30."

I jumped up, gathering the blanket around me as I grabbed my jeans from the arm of a chair. "Sorry, I'll get out of your way. You probably need to get ready for work."

She laughed. "Jeremy, it's Saturday."

I sat back down on the couch. "Oh, yeah. That's a relief. I would have gotten out, but you probably would have found me collapsed someplace in your parking lot."

Then, looking at me, she said, "I'm sorry. I should have found you a pair of shorts to sleep in. They would have to be more comfortable than sleeping in your underwear."

"Yeah, right, you have something in my size," I teased. But then, I realized, I knew nothing about her. There could be lots of reasons why she would have shorts in my size, one of the more pressing in my mind being whether they belonged to a boyfriend who occasionally stayed over. I was tempted to try to work the question into the conversation, but was spared that decision when she continued.

"You'd be surprised. I love baggy clothes to sleep in. How about some breakfast?"

I was glad she was changing the topic because talking about what she wore to bed would have made it difficult for me to think of ... well, anything other than what she wore to bed. I knew I needed to interject some realism into my fantasies. She was a beautiful, successful doctor and I was what? Still growing up?

"Now that I think about the options for breakfast," Diane said, "you can have anything you want, as long as it's something swimming in milk." She headed toward the kitchen, walking so near to me that I could feel the warmth of her passing.

"Great. I love my eggs Benedict swimming in milk."

"Very funny," she replied, turning around. "I just never found the time to learn to cook, but I can pour a mean bowl of cereal."

"You're in luck. Cooking was one skill my mom made sure I learned. I'm not certain, but I think she was worried that I'd never find anyone willing to do it for me. Care if I check the fridge?"

She shrugged. "Not at all."

I went to investigate and when I came back into the living room, she was coming down the stairs again, this time with the vest in hand. "I forgot this. I was pretty sure you were still asleep, so I finished it up earlier this morning."

"Looks great. I doubt there'd be any scar if you closed a guy's gut with that stitching." She smiled, seeming proud of her handiwork.

"How about a veggie Denver omelet?" I asked. "You have onions, peppers, and cheese, but I didn't see any ham or bacon."

"Sure." She perched herself on a stool at the island in her kitchen, as I went to work.

"Coffee?" I asked.

"Only if you make it strong."

"I do. Enough so that if you need to cut it with some hot water, just say the word."

It only took a few minutes to whip up breakfast, and soon, we were seated side-by-side at the island with a mug of steaming coffee and a plate overflowing with omelet in front of us. She took a sip of coffee, then a bite of omelet. Then, the pattern repeated. I was starting to wonder if the coffee was too strong, or the omelet too spicy. I had slipped in a bit of salsa, just before I served them.

"Jeremy, you could spoil a girl with breakfasts like these. This is absolutely wonderful."

I grinned, basking in her praise, even if it was just breakfast. "My pleasure." I couldn't remember the last time I had cooked for anyone else. Riley, my ex-girlfriend was a toast and coffee person for breakfast, if that. So, a big breakfast on a Saturday morning was a rarity for me.

We ate in silence for a while, neither of us apparently uneasy with the quiet. For me, I was becoming lost in a warm and homey feeling. It was something that I had not felt in some time, maybe not since my parents had died over eight years ago.

That, of course, was admitting quite a bit to myself, since for nearly four of those eight years, I had been living with Riley. But she was more the candle-burning at both ends kind of person. She was always on the go. It had been exciting, at least for a while. But it had also become much of the reason we had gone our separate ways.

This sense of belonging, of being at home that I felt here was something that I missed more than I knew. When this was all over, I told myself, I'd have to see if I could recapture this feeling and put my life on a path I could embrace, rather than just tread robotically.

But at this moment, Diane and I still had problems we needed to solve. And she was evidently more task-focused than I, because she said, "I was thinking about what we should say to Detective Underwood."

"And?"

"Well, I'm not certain we need to tell him anything other than a couple of thugs came after us at the mall, and when we fled on your bike, one of them crashed. It's just, I don't know how you give him the GPS tracker without explaining where you got it. And that explanation involves mentioning the vest."

"I guess we could just drop it on a long-haul truck and let Jones chase it to Boise and back," I joked. "But that wouldn't get him closer to jail and out of our lives. Maybe I could just tell Underwood that I think Jones planted it on me. Or maybe, in my car, when I was working at the lab."

"That's not bad," said Diane. She paused a moment more in thought. "I can't think of any other sticking points. You?"

"No, not really. Since Jones is being so persistent, Underwood might take my walking-through-walls story more seriously. But even if he doesn't, the guy and his pal tried to assault us. I think we're ready."

I made a call to the department, just to confirm that Underwood would be there, and we left. We went by the spot where I had left my car and switched to it. Today, it was too cold to be on the bike.

△ △ △

"Dr. Stapleton, it's nice to meet you," said Underwood, after I did the introductions. Then, he peered at me closely through his wire-rims, as he gave the knot in his tie a tug. "And you're looking better than the last time."

"I've had good care," I replied, wondering if the statement implied more than I intended. But Diane seemed to take no notice and Underwood merely nodded.

Turning back to Diane, Underwood said, "So, from the voicemail that Jeremy left, it sounds like you had the misfortune to meet this Jones character yesterday at the mall on Gavelton Road?"

"Yes. We were inside the mall when they accosted us, threatened us with baseball bats."

"They? There was more than one person?" asked Underwood.

"Yeah," I replied. "Jones brought a friend with him this time."

"And baseball bats? No gun?"

"No, bats," I confirmed.

Underwood typed something into his computer. "And they actually threatened you?"

I think that question bothered Diane a little, as she jumped back into the conversation, completely in doctor mode. "Absolutely. Jones specifically used the phrase, 'beat you to a pulp.' There was no doubt that they meant to harm us."

"OK," said Underwood. "I just wanted to establish that this was an attempted assault, rather than just some type of misunderstanding." But he obviously wasn't finished questioning this assertion. "Wouldn't attacking someone in a mall with a baseball bat be a little … indiscreet?"

"It's the mall," I said. "There are people walking around with all kinds of things. A bat wouldn't stick out at all. And besides, we were in a wing where most of the shops were being renovated, so there weren't that many people around."

"You were shopping in an area with no stores?" Underwood sounded somewhat doubtful. I could feel Diane tense up again. It was clear, she didn't like his skepticism.

"We weren't there shopping," I clarified for the detective. "We were mostly just talking, so a quieter spot was perfect."

Detective Underwood now turned fully toward me and leaned forward. "Are you certain this was Jones?" he asked. "I mean, now there are two people and they are using a different weapon. That's all possible, of course, but that much change in the attackers and their tactics is a bit unusual."

"I'm absolutely certain. We weren't that far apart— maybe 10 or 15 feet. It was definitely Jones." I sat back in the chair and reached into my pocket, thinking that now was the perfect time to give the detective the key to solving this case.

"And besides, I have a foolproof way for you to catch him. He'll come to you."

Underwood looked puzzled. I held the tracker up for him to see. "Jones planted this device on me ... in my car. It's a GPS tracker. I think if you just power it up, some place public where I might be, he'll show up. Then, you can grab him."

"Interesting," said Underwood, as he took the tracker and turned it over in his hands.

"I thought you might think so." But my self-satisfaction was shaken a bit as the detective wasn't smiling.

"That's not exactly what I meant. It's just interesting that someone who was supposedly working with technology that did the impossible would use something so low tech. My brother-in-law has these on his delivery trucks, so he knows how his drivers are coming on their routes. I think they're only accurate to 20 feet or so."

"But it would still get Jones close enough to spot me," I pointed out.

"You, or your car?" asked Underwood.

"Well, the car, but I'm often in it." I didn't like even this small fib about the tracker's location, wondering if the deceit was showing in my face. I fidgeted in my chair, scratching at a spot on my cheek that didn't really itch.

"How did you find this tracker?" asked Underwood, rubbing his chin. "They're pretty small, and not that easy to see."

"I just stumbled on it." Another layer of white lies. I wondered if they were bothering Diane too, as I felt her shift in her chair next to me.

"That was lucky, wasn't it?" said Underwood, raising his eyebrows just a bit. I was sure he thought there was more to this story than I was telling him, but I couldn't change the details now.

"So, to set up this sting to catch Jones in a public area, as you put it, we'll need to spot him when he arrives," said Underwood. "Assuming the person Santiago rented the lab to was Jones, we have his description and yours. According to the composite, he's a white male, 25-35 years old, 6 foot 2 to 6 foot 4 inches, 210 to 240 pounds, brown hair, somewhat wavy, cut short, right-handed, no tattoos, no birthmarks."

"Yeah, I know," I said. "We've been through this. There's nothing distinguishing in our descriptions."

"Don't get me wrong," said Underwood. "The two of you were more consistent than most eyewitnesses. But assuming this guy checks out the area before he walks into this trap, we'd need to be watching every spot that has a line of sight. By definition of a public area, we could end up with a couple of dozen potential suspects. Or more."

I guess my foolproof scheme wasn't quite as good as I had hoped. I gave Diane a sideways glance. She continued to look forward, but slipped her hand over below the level of the desk and placed it on mine. I appreciated the show of support. We had given it a shot, but clearly, neither of us were law enforcement professionals.

"Look, I'll give it some more thought. Maybe I can come up with something. OK?" asked the detective.

"Thanks," I replied.

"Then, after these threats, you and Dr. Stapleton ran from the mall and they pursued you?" asked Underwood.

"Correct," I replied, glad that we had moved on. "We got on my motorcycle, and they got into their cars. I went north on Gavelton, then right on Billingsley Road. They followed."

"There's a sign at Gavelton and Billingsley saying that the street is closed for repairs. Why'd you take it?" asked Underwood.

"We're on a motorcycle. They're in cars. What better place is there to lose them?"

"I guess. But I checked the photos from the crash, and there's no space on the shoulder to get around that roadblock."

"It was tight," was all I said.

Underwood cocked his head, frowning. If he was opening the door for me to claim I could pass through solid objects, and therefore, be able to dismiss me again, I wasn't taking the bait. But even if he could question just about all of our story, there was one fact that was undeniable.

"I guess you have the body from the crash. Doesn't that prove we were being chased?"

Underwood looked at us for a moment, his eyes traveling back and forth. "Yes, we have a body recovered from the crash. But that section of Billingsley Road is remote enough that it has been the site of quite a bit of street racing. This is not the first crash in that area, although it's the first fatality. And strangely, the call to report the crash wasn't from you. In fact, your call to my voicemail was nearly an hour and a half later. By that time, the accident had already been reported and had even made the news."

I sat up straighter in my chair. "Are you saying, I heard about the crash and now, I'm using it to support my claims about Jones?" I asked. My voice rose a notch, in the heat of the accusation. I felt a slight squeeze from Diane's hand.

"No, Jeremy, I'm saying there are a lot of theories that fit the facts. And one of those possibilities is that you have some beef with Jones, and when the first set of claims against him seemed to dead end, you came up with another. I hope that's not the case, especially as you have now involved someone else." Underwood nodded toward Diane as he made the last statement.

Diane had obviously had enough, as her light touch on my hand turned to a firm grip. Out of the corner of my eye, I could see her sit up, ram-rod straight in her chair. "Detective, I'm not some impressionable school girl. The individual that Jeremy addressed as Tom threatened us, and chased us until his friend crashed into the roadblock. You can take all that information as fact."

How Detective Underwood sifted so quickly through all this verbiage and found a loose end to pull surprised me. "Are you saying that Jones never introduced himself?" he asked.

Diane hesitated, apparently trying to recall this specific detail. "Jeremy addressed him as Thomas Jones, and Jones didn't say anything like, why are you calling me that?"

Underwood did his trademark 'wait in silence for the witness to give more details,' but Diane said nothing. Finally, he asked, "But he didn't give his name?"

Diane slid even further toward the edge of her seat. Her hand left mine and she gripped the arm of her chair tightly. I returned her earlier gesture, and lightly placed my hand on hers. I could feel her relax, but only a bit. "No, he didn't say, my name is Thomas Jones."

I figured Underwood knew his business, but I still had visions of this exchange spiraling out of control, not that I would have blamed Diane. It had to be tough being the innocent bystander when the police are not quite sure if they should believe you or not.

Just then, Underwood's phone rang. "Excuse me, I need to get this."

After a moment on the line, he hung up and turned back to us. "Jeremy, Diane, I need to apologize if you think I was giving you a hard time. I was just trying to get the facts."

"Thanks, I understand," I said. But actually, I didn't. I didn't know what to make of his words. And I was even less sure Diane accepted the apology, as she continued to stare at the detective without saying a word.

"The body from the crash has been positively identified as Thomas R. Jones," continued Underwood. "This will allow us to close the case, assuming there is no evidence of foul play. He won't be bothering you anymore."

Diane and I turned and gaped at each other, bewildered. Then I spoke. "That's not possible. Jones was in the second car, the one that didn't crash. He's still alive."

"Alive? Are you certain?" asked Underwood.

I glanced at Diane again, just to confirm that her memory agreed with mine. I received a slight nod in return. "Yes, Detective, I'm positive."

"So, you believe there were two individuals named Tom Jones after you?" For an individual who to this point had never seemed perturbed, Underwood sounded a bit exasperated. But if he was slightly so, I was even more. I felt like Jones had me running in circles.

"No, I don't think the individual that I knew from the lab on Collingsway is really Thomas Jones. I don't know what his real name is, but he did threaten us with ball bats. He took a shot at me back at the lab. And he's still alive." This all came out, rapid-fire.

"So, I've got two people, both with aliases, working in a lab that the owner claims was empty. And they work for a company that doesn't exist. And they're either working on something you can't tell me about or something so preposterous it would have been better had you not told me. And finally, we have the body of someone you say was chasing you and that has the name you've given me repeatedly, but now it's not the person at the lab?"

OK, maybe Underwood was more than a little exasperated, as his voice escalated as he counted off his frustrations. But he was still calmer than I.

I gritted my teeth. "It's a bitch," I said bluntly, "but that's the truth."

"We'll be in contact if we get any additional leads." I could tell by the way he bit off the words that this was Underwood's final statement.

As we were leaving the building and heading back to my car, Diane took my hand and said, "That could have gone better."

"He's decided this is just a red herring," I said, stating the obvious.

"Yes, I think we've heard his decision—that this has something to do with a disagreement between you and Jones. And you're using the police to get revenge on him. Maybe he thinks there are other possibilities, but I doubt he is actively checking any of them."

She stopped walking, so I turned to look at her. Her face was still slightly flushed from the meeting. "Are you certain you don't want to turn on the vest and go marching back into his office without opening the door?"

I took a deep breath, trying for rationality rather than momentary satisfaction. "I'd love to, but I don't think so. Like you said, he's probably not going to do much, so we really need to hang onto the vest for our own protection. And when we find Schmidt and get it back to him, that gets us out of this bind, too."

She squeezed my hand and nodded. She looked at the sidewalk a moment, then back up at me. "So, I guess it's clear I have a bit of a temper."

I shrugged. "I actually think you showed a great deal of restraint," I said, meaning it. She nodded, smiling at me. We turned and left for the car, now certain we were on our own.

10. Off the grid

wondered if going by the mall to get Diane's car was too much of a risk. But after we sat in the parking lot for an hour and saw nothing suspicious, we took the chance. I trailed her home, just to be sure no one was following.

"I didn't see a thing on the way here," I said to Diane, meeting her on the sidewalk in front of her home. "I think you'll be fine."

"Did you call me as we were driving back? I don't answer the phone while I'm driving. As a doctor, I get to see too many people who do."

I gave her a nod in agreement. "Yeah, I stay off the phone when I driving, too. And frankly, I didn't expect you to answer. But since it's probably safe to use mine, I grabbed it from the trunk and gave you a call. Thought you should have my number, just in case."

She cocked an eye at me questioningly.

"Yeah, I glanced at the number on your phone, when I was making breakfast," answering what I was certain was her question.

She flashed a knowing smile, stating "That must be nice to have."

"What's that?"

"Photographic memory." She hid a soft laugh behind her hand, but the amusement in her eyes was unmistakable.

"OK, guilty. Maybe it was more than a glance," I admitted, glad I was caught. "I was afraid when I head out of here in a few minutes, I'd never see you again. I mean, without accidentally getting a flat tire in front of your place. Calling's a little less ... obvious."

She dropped her hand from her face and smiled at me openly. I knew I wasn't a teenager, but I swear I felt weak in the knees. "You didn't have to worry," she said. "I already programmed your number into my phone. I actually saw your name pop up when you called, but I thought I'd give you a hard time."

"Mission accomplished." It would have been nice to stand there flirting all morning—I could really think of nothing I'd like more—but I was homeless again and needed to start thinking about a more permanent solution to Mr. Jones. "So, be careful," I said. "Lock the doors and don't open them without checking."

"Are you going somewhere? Surely, not back to your apartment."

"Well, maybe for a second, just to grab a few things. And not before I watch the place for a good long time and make certain no one's hiding out there. Then, I'm going to drop off the grid. Live off the land, using nothing but cash. Change my routine every day and wear disguises."

Diane laughed, the light mood of a moment ago returning. "So now you're the spy, Jeremy Reynolds ... if that's really your name? Seriously, what's your plan?"

I kicked at a small stone laying on the sidewalk, knowing fully that I didn't have one. "Well, after I grab a few more of my things, I'll probably check into some really cheap motel. Without the GPS tracker giving away my location, I should be safe anywhere except my apartment or the lab. And I guess Jones might watch the police station, from time to time."

"What about parents, or brothers, or sisters. Anyone you can stay with?"

"My parents passed away, and I have no brothers or sisters."

"Oh, I'm sorry about your folks." There was a soft sympathy in her voice.

"That's OK. It's been a while. Anyway, I figure I'll continue to hunt for Jones, Schmidt, or his company. Find any of them, and we're out of the woods." I gave her a grin, trying to appear positive about the outcome although I wasn't yet.

Diane paused a moment, reaching out to place her hand softly on my arm. It was both attention-grabbing and distracting at the same time, but I did listen well enough to hear her say, "This isn't a long-term solution, but do you want to stay here for a few days? If we've missed something that will tip-off Jones, it's likely he'll find it sooner rather than later. And if he does, I'd like to have you nearby."

"And the vest nearby, too," I said, mentally bounding my elation with some reality.

"Yes," she nodded. "And the vest, too. But mostly you."

I was still trying to process the totally unexpected accolade when she shifted back to the practical. "Why don't you go do your surveillance and grab your stuff. That'll give me a chance to straighten up."

"I've been enough trouble already," I said.

"Jeremy, you need to stop saying that. It's no trouble. If I was in your place, I would be doing the same as you."

"You would have gone looking for a part-time accountant to crash at his place for a couple of days?"

"Very funny," she groaned, and she gave me a playful push toward my car. "Now, get out of here before I decide I can't live with your sense of humor."

It was the nicest, fake reprimand I had ever received.

△ △ △

When I returned to Diane's with a roller bag stuffed with clothes and toiletries in hand, I decided I did not understand the concept of 'straightening up.' She had removed an end table and a small magazine stand from the space near the couch. In their place were two small chests of drawers. At least they were mismatched, because the statement, 'it's no trouble' was becoming harder for me to accept by the minute.

"This chest," she was saying, "has a few towels, extra sheets, and the like. You can put your things in the other. Last night, you looked too tired to care, but the couch folds out. I put clean sheets on it."

"Diane, this is really nice of you."

She smiled. "You may have your own in the roller, but if not, do you think these will fit?" She held up a pair of shorts that had to be close to twice her size.

"Yes, I'd guess they would. Since I didn't want to waste the space on PJs, I'll gladly accept. But truthfully, you couldn't possibly wear those without them falling to your knees."

"Why do you think I wore a smaller pair this morning?" she said with a shy smile.

With the images it was bringing to mind, I was more than a little interested in continuing the current dialog when she again shifted to the practical. "Are you planning on just waiting to see if Jones has disappeared, or do something more active to find out?"

"Good question," I said, rubbing my chin. "I expected to be in the wait-and-see mode for a while, but then, I thought I'd be spending a lot of time figuring out how to live out of a suitcase. Since that's not an issue, maybe I should see what I can do to find him."

"I think you should," she said. "With an actual person, and me to verify that he physically threatened us, the police would have a hard time looking the other way."

"We just need to make sure we don't tip him off that we're looking. Getting chased all over south St. Louis is getting old. When I did some checking at the library, before I stumbled on your name, I thought I might be able to find him through Schmidt. But I couldn't find Schmidt either. So then, I tried to find some companies or university departments that might have bankrolled Schmidt's research, and came up with four possibilities."

"Like who?" she asked.

"The list's still on my laptop." I grabbed it out of my bag, sat down at the kitchen island, and fired it up. Diane came over and we switched places at the computer.

"Frontier Atomics," she read aloud from the screen. "Of course, they do quite a bit of high-tech stuff, all of which would be at least trade secret. Some of it would even be classified. You found my name while you were doing these searches?"

"I don't remember the exact keywords, but yeah. What I found was some type of public interest article, about you becoming a country doctor."

She laughed. "Country doctor. Yeah, I remember that story. The writer was originally from New York City and thought anything west of New Jersey was the country."

She paused, turning from the screen to look up at me as if she expected me to say something, but I had no idea what. Finally, I just said, "Yeah, I hear New Yorkers can be that way."

After connecting my laptop to her wireless, she did a couple of searches, treading the same virtual space I had previously. I thought about saying it was wasted effort when she said, "Did you see this stuff about quantum tunneling?"

"No, I didn't." I leaned down to read over her shoulder. While the article was technical in places, it also had several sections suitable for the general public—me. And while it made clear that its language was misleading by necessity, the analogy it used was a ball passing through a wall rather than bouncing off it.

I stood up straight, staring at the wall across the kitchen, dumbstruck. When I found my voice, I said, "I can't imagine how I missed that. It could well be the starting point for the vest."

Diane turned again, looking up. "Possibly. If nothing else, it fits with what Jones said. And it's one more, really strange circumstance that resulted in us meeting because I can't imagine you'd come find me after reading this."

I drew back, surprised at her comment. I bent down again, reading more closely. She was right. I had no trouble seeing there was virtually no overlap between the words on the screen and the little I knew about nuclear medicine. "Strange? No kidding." It was all I could think to say.

Diane turned back to the laptop and surfed to Frontier Atomics home page. Then, she started going through their press releases and project descriptions.

"I did that at the library, but the descriptions were too vague for me to come up with anything."

"Same here," she said. "Half of these make it sound like Frontier Atomics is just a step away from achieving world peace and ending global hunger."

"Their webpage does give me one idea," I said, as I bent down again to read over her shoulder. "It looks like they give tours, including Saturday afternoons. I know, it's not like they'll have one of these vests in a display case in the entry hall, but I've seen everything this vest holds. If there was even a box or a component that looked the same, we might be able to narrow our search to one company and maybe even one department. After that, I think we'd have a good shot at finding Schmidt."

She smiled at me, nodding. "Sounds like a plan. Let's go."

"Us?"

"Of course. You got a glimpse at the electronics when I dumped some of them out on the table at that restaurant. But I worked with all of that stuff for a couple of hours, when I was sewing the new one. And besides, the vest looks a little bulky on you. I'll tighten it up around my waist and no one will know the difference. No, if only one of us is going, it should be me."

I shook my head and smiled at how easily she had turned the tables on me. "I think we can both make the trip."

She stood up from the island, patted me on the shoulder, and said, "Good choice. I'm going to get ready."

11. Hubby gets a clue

I f the press releases on Frontier Atomics' website were carefully phrased window-dressing, then the words coming from our tour guide's mouth were the masterpiece from which they had been drawn. But even so, the technology behind the drivel was awe-inspiring. The companies Frontier supported were a veritable Who's Who in alternative energy, artificial intelligence and robotics, aerospace, and agriculture. And of course, Diane's field, nuclear medicine, was also well represented. While their name never seemed to be on the outside of any of the products their clients developed, under the hood, their handiwork was often at the heart.

"This stuff is amazing," I whispered to Diane, as our tour group shuffled along the hall, peering into one lab after another.

She gave me that quizzical look I had seen on her face from time to time but still didn't understand. Then, it disappeared and she said, "It is. But what we're seeing is carefully choreographed. The medical equipment we just saw was all early version technology, at least one and sometimes two generations old. The real cutting-edge stuff, where the vest would be if it's here at all, must be buried inside, behind closed doors."

"Well, like you said, inventors have to protect their discoveries."

"Sure," Diane agreed. "I guess it was asking too much for anything related to the vest or quantum tunneling to show up on a tour like this. Or even related capabilities ... whatever those might be."

Something our guide said caught Diane's ear. I didn't notice what it was exactly, because I was too busy watching her face.

"Ah, and here we are at one area where Frontier should have just minded their own business," she said, a touch of ire creeping into her voice. "It's their research on electrophoresis."

"You mean that process that separates particles using an electric field?" I asked.

Diane stared at me, apparently more than a little surprised by my response. Actually, I was too, as I hadn't thought about anything like this in years.

"Yeah, that process. Accounting give you a lot of exposure to electrophoresis?" she asked, tilting her head in a questioning fashion.

"It's a long story. But it can't be as interesting as why you dislike Frontier because of their research on it."

"Well, that's obvious," she said with that twinkle in her eye that let me know this was going to be anything but straightforward. "You know who Charles Walker is?"

"No, I don't think so," I replied.

"He was a St. Louis-based, United States astronaut. In the mid-1980s, he flew missions to perfect electrophoresis in space. The basic idea was that the process might work better if the effect of gravity on the particles was removed.

It could have been the first major manufacturing factory in space." Her tempo and tone increased with each sentence, as she warmed to a topic that was clearly close to her heart.

"Until Frontier upset those plans?" I asked, somewhat tentatively.

"Right, until they and their counterparts did. They kept working on the process on the ground until what Charlie was doing in orbit became irrelevant. How great would it have been, to have St. Louis-developed technology circling the earth in the first space factory? I'll never forgive Frontier for interfering."

"Charlie, huh? On a first-name basis, are you?"

Diane laughed. "Are you jealous? Don't be. I don't think I was even born until his last flights, but I remember reading about it when I was a teen. I guess I was a bit of a nerd, huh?"

"A very cute one, no doubt."

Diane seemed to have this effect on me, where I was saying the first thing that popped into my mind. It wasn't at all like me, where words came only after careful analysis. But if that was surprising, her reaction was even more so. She looked embarrassed by the compliment, as she gave me a shy smile, then seemed to be studying her shoes.

I also realized, that if she had been born in the mid-1980s when Charles Walker was working in space, she was as young as she looked. Altogether, her beauty, brains, and at least partial attraction to me were a bit mind-boggling and I wondered if I was mistaken. Perhaps I was just riding the wave of adrenaline from the events of the past few days?

When I looked up, I realized that our group had continued around the corner. "You know, there's a way we can check out what they have behind those closed doors."

Diane looked puzzled for only a second, then asked, "You don't mean use the vest, do you?"

"We brought it for a reason, didn't we?" I asked, raising my eyebrows.

"We brought it because we both agreed to keep it close as long as Jones was still out there," Diane replied. "I didn't think you were going all industrial spy on me."

"I'm just saying, we could stick our head through a wall, take a quick look. No one would be the wiser. But the trouble is, I don't know where we should be taking these peeks, and it might be a bit obvious if we walked along with our heads on the other side of the wall."

"You think?" she joked.

"So, maybe you can pick out a few doors where we might have a chance at finding something?"

Diane still looked a bit doubtful. "Whatever the vest is doing, it's way over my head. And as we've both seen, no lab door so far has said quantum tunneling." I took a page from Underwood's book and waited to see if she might talk herself into trying. "I guess the door we just passed on the other side of the hall caught my interest. It said 'Mechanosynthesis,' and it was one of just a handful of doors that have been closed."

"I guess I missed the day in accounting school where they discussed that one."

"Not surprising. As far as I know, it's still hypothetical. It has to do with using extremely small machines to force atoms or molecules to attach to each other in precise ways.

It's sort of like parking cars in every spot in a parking lot in order to make one specific car take the only remaining opening."

"And you think the vest could be affecting atoms that way when we pass through?"

"No, I still think what the vest does is impossible. But after I throw out all the technologies that I know absolutely nothing about, which by the way covers most of the doors we've passed, mechanosynthesis is the best of what's left."

"Good enough for me. Shall we take a peek?" I asked as I wagged my head in the direction of the lab.

We stepped across the hall and back down the corridor about 10 yards to the appropriate door. Diane flipped on the power switch, grabbed my hand, and together, we stepped into the lab. I have to admit that my first impression was ... disappointment.

"It looks like they're tearing it down, maybe moving on to some new project," Diane said. "I wonder if that's what's happening behind each of the closed doors? They're just projects that are ending."

"Good to know. If nothing else, that'll help us reduce the number of places to look. Shall we find the next candidate?"

"Just a second. There's a notebook over there." And she started for it. It was only about 10 feet away, but even before she got there, two men burst into the room. Both were carrying firearms, but I guess by policy, neither had drawn them yet. Their hands, however, were resting near the holsters.

"Please keep your hands where we can see them and move to the outside wall," one of them commanded.

Diane and I did not need to act in order to look startled.

"What's going on?" I managed to ask. "We're on a tour." Realizing that the badge that we were required to wear had flipped over sometime earlier, I reached up toward my pocket to correct it.

Their guns flew out of the holsters in what had to be an often-practiced maneuver. For the second time in three days, I was staring down the barrel of a gun. While the previous time the shooter had missed, I had no confidence that this one would, since he was only about six feet away.

"I'm just trying to show you my badge," I said.

"Sir, you're in a closed area. Make no moves other than to raise your hands and back up to the wall behind you." I did so, finding Diane already there.

"Please turn and face the wall and place your hands on it, above your head."

When we were in position, one guard stepped forward and said, "Sir, I'm going to search you for weapons. Please don't make any sudden moves or I'll be forced to restrain you."

"OK, but I have nothing on me," I replied.

He confirmed it thoroughly and a bit roughly, but I can't say I blamed him. There were too many shootings of security and law enforcement personnel to handle any situation casually.

When he was done, he said, "Ma'am, there'll be a female officer here shortly to search you."

Diane said, "Don't get fresh and we can get it over with now. I can't stand here forever with my hands up."

I guess their female officers were in short supply because after glancing at his counterpart, the guard said "Cancel Robinson" into some type of microphone clipped to his collar. Then, after he had committed to the process, Diane said, "Just don't be too rough. I'm three months pregnant."

I gagged, then started coughing to cover my slipup. "Sorry, allergies," I said, remembering too late that it was early November. But the guards took no notice, probably because they were too worried about searching a pregnant woman.

The guard barely touched Diane and after a few moments, declared she was unarmed. If he felt any lumps under the sweater she was wearing over the vest, he said nothing.

After asking our names and taking our driver's licenses, the guard who had searched us opened the door to the lab and stepped into the hallway to read our names into the microphone. There was some conversation, back and forth, but I couldn't make out the details. After a few more minutes, he stepped back inside and looked at Diane. "Are you any relation to Dr. George Stapleton?"

"I'm his daughter."

The guard stepped out again, followed by more muted talk. After about five minutes, a third man stepped in. He was much older than the guards and was dressed in a white lab coat. He held out his hand to Diane.

"I'm Dr. Larry Russell, director of our nanotechnology research department. When I heard the name Dr. Stapleton, I thought it was your dad ... until they said your first name, of course. I know your dad. He's a good man, very supportive of the work we've been doing here."

Diane didn't blink an eye and merely extended her hand. "Dr. Russell, nice to meet you. This is Mr. Jeremy Reynolds. I have to say, Dr. Russell, this tour has been ... different.

When we saw the open door, we stepped in for a look. The next thing you know, men with guns have us surrounded and I'm being searched for weapons."

Dr. Russell looked stricken. He gave the guards an icy stare before his eyes returned to Diane with a look of sympathy. Most likely seeing that his reaction was a bit stronger than she wanted, Diane added, "Don't get me wrong, we both greatly admire the work of law enforcement, Jeremy and I. It's a tough job, and potentially dangerous."

Good, I'm not going to end up on the wrong side of two men with guns.

"It's just a bit frightening how efficient they are," Diane concluded. I would have nominated her for an Emmy on the spot.

"Yes, our security forces are some of the best trained in the industry," Russell said. "Can you wait here for a moment?" Then, he and one of the guards went into the hall, followed by more indistinguishable chatter.

When he returned, Russell said, "To make up for this slight misunderstanding, would you be interested in a short, personal tour? I'd be honored if you and your husband have the time."

"Oh, I'm not ...." I had no chance to finish my statement.

"That's OK, honey," Diane said to me. "We can push back our later engagement." I nearly gagged again but caught myself this time. Then, turning back to Russell, Diane said, "We'd be happy to join you."

For the next 45 minutes, I followed Diane and one of the two security guards on Russell's personal tour of the facility. I kept up with some of the talk, but if anyone was going to make a connection between the vest and the research at Frontier, it would be Diane, not me.

So, I gravitated to the guard, Officer Lowell Frankie. At first, he was very apologetic. Most likely, offending a VIP was career-limiting at Frontier, although it was really Diane's father who was the VIP. The family connection, however, was working in our favor. And Frankie had also heard Diane voicing respect for his career field, so he soon moved on to small talk.

Like me, he was a big fan of college basketball, and as a new season had just started, we spent most of the tour talking about the prospects of the local teams—St. Louis University and the universities of Missouri and Illinois. Generally, we agreed to disagree, which was common among sports fans. But disagreements on sports is actually more of a bond than an obstacle.

When we returned to the area outside his office, Russell said to Diane, "Can I show you something your father gave me?"

Diane glanced at me. "Sure, go ahead, sugar," I said. "I'll hang here with Officer Frankie until you're done."

After they entered the office, I turned to Frankie. "I still think you're selling Mizzou short, what with the new coach being in his third year. They'll do better than most think."

"We'll see," the guard replied, acting as if he knew something no one else did.

"Hey, I've been racking my brain for a name the whole time we've been here. Diane and I met someone the other day that may work for Frontier. He ran a lab down south, in Robertsville."

"Nope, no way he works here. No one works off-site."

"Sure, tight security on all this stuff, huh?"

"Absolutely. I guess he could have been here some other time. These docs come and go with the funding. What's he look like?"

I described Schmidt, who unlike Jones, had a host of distinguishing features ... at least in an almost stereotypical fashion. He was, to me, the image of a European doctor, with a heavy accent, thinning gray hair, gray beard and mustache, and dark-rimmed glasses surrounding brown, penetrating eyes. Even his manner of dress fit my stereotype, right down to the tweed jackets with leather on the elbows that he favored.

"That sounds like Benzinger. That's Dr. Nils Benzinger." Frankie looked around as if he was about to divulge a national secret. "He's not really held in very high regard around here. Took a bunch of money. Was rarely in his lab, though he spent it all. Then, he ended up with almost nothing to show."

"So, he's gone now?" I asked.

"Yeah, gone from Frontier, but I think he's still in St. Louis. I thought I heard something about him just the other day."

I wanted to ask, was it something about his murder as I was still wondering why Jones was giving us all his attention and overlooking Schmidt/Benzinger. Or was Benzinger working with Jones, in which case the news might have been something like fund-raising to build the world headquarters of the Environmental Barrier empire? But even that goal seemed much too pedestrian, as the vest could be so much more than the better storm door.

"This is a pretty big place," I said to Frankie. "You keep up on all the researchers?"

"Naw. Hardly know any of them. But the lab with the malfunctioning door, it's in my area. And what's even stranger, it was Benzinger's, till he got booted about eight weeks ago."

It had already become a 'malfunctioning door,' rather than one that had been left open. Whatever worked best for the guards worked for me.

"Yeah, that is strange we ended up in his old lab," I said. "Thanks for keeping me company. Sports gossip beats tech-talk any time. As for Benzinger, I'll have to see what the little woman has to say about him." I was starting to enjoy the husband and wife act, even if it was only going to last as far as the front door.

"Yeah, you scored big catching that one," Frankie said, winking conspiratorially. "Beauty and brains and about to be a dad."

"Yeah, that came as a big surprise to me," I said, just as Diane emerged from Russell's office.

I nodded good-bye to Frankie and turned to Diane. "All ready to go, sugar?"

As we descended the steps outside Frontier, Diane said, "Well, you certainly got into that role fast. All ready to go, sugar?" She laughed.

"Just following your lead. And by the way, why didn't you correct him rather than making me your fake husband and soon-to-be-father of our child?"

"Who said it's yours?" I groaned as she grinned at me. "I was hoping we'd get access to some of their more closely held work. If so, spouses might get to come along. But friends—no way. Unfortunately, what we ended up seeing was pretty much public fare. Generally, the visit was a bust."

"Maybe not. I think we should check out one Dr. Nils Benzinger."

"Who's that?" Diane asked, suddenly serious.

"Turns out your woman's intuition was hitting on all cylinders. You picked his lab to investigate, that Mechanosynthesis thing. He's gone. Apparently misspent his funding and left about eight weeks ago, according to the guard. But the best part? He fits Schmidt's description to a T."

"Nice work, honey," she said, putting her arm around my shoulders, and we headed back to her place.

12. The vanishing man

I looked over my shoulder at Diane. "Definitely, that's him. That's Dr. Johannes Schmidt." I was online, looking at his webpage. "Didn't I tell you? We have a middle-aged Sigmund Freud living in St. Louis."

"You weren't kidding." She stepped away from the computer to retrieve her drink from the kitchen.

I scrolled down the page, reading the data I found there loud enough for her to hear in the next room. "Swiss quantum physicist, now living in the United States. Looks like his primary research has been on space travel. That's outer space, as opposed to space inside an atom." Then, more quietly, I said to myself, "Interesting."

"What's interesting?" asked Diane. She had chosen that exact moment to return to the living room.

"Schmidt ... or Benzinger, I guess it is. Anyway, he's been working on those quantum vacuum plasma thrusters. You ever hear of them?"

"Nope, never. But it sounds like you have."

"What can I say. I'm curious. And for the curious, quantum vacuum plasma thrusters are mind candy. They're supposed to collect some type of particles that occur in space and use them to create thrust. It's so strange that a lot of people call them 'anomalous thrust devices.' You think there's any chance quantum tunneling and this space travel research morphed into the vest?"

Diane covered her mouth to hide a laugh, saying, "And to think, I described myself as a nerd, when, honey, you have me beat by a mile. I have no idea."

Since the husband and wife ruse at Frontier Atomics, she had thrown my nickname into our dialog a few times, always teasing. Nonetheless, I was still forgetting to breathe each time she did.

"Yeah, if you put a Star Wars movie on, I'd probably find something in it that became the vest too. I'm going to see what Benzinger's been up to recently," I said.

Diane came back over and stationed herself behind me. Laying a hand on my shoulder, she bent closer to read the screen. I found myself reading the same sentences, over and over, as my mind kept wandering back to the warmth of her touch.

"Looks like your guard friend Frankie was right," Diane said. "Benzinger's still in St. Louis, and pretty visible too. Look at that ...."

"What?" I focused, hoping to catch up with her on the page.

"He's going to be at the St. Louis Science Center, tomorrow afternoon, as part of a panel on the future of space travel," she said, pointing at a link about two-thirds of the way down the page.

"And there's a reception for the panel afterward," I saw, once I caught up. "Sounds like the perfect time to ask him a few questions about his business. And, about Jones."

Diane frowned. "It might be, but it's members only. I should be a member of the Science Center, but I'm not.".

I turned to look at her. "No worries. I am." Diane got that puzzled look of hers again. "What?" I asked.

She hesitated a moment longer, then shrugged and said, "It's nothing."

Even though I had not known her long, I was certain there was no point pushing it. When she wanted to know, she'd ask. She was that kind of person.

I shut down the laptop and went to sit on the couch. Diane joined me, sitting with her legs tucked under her in a way that caused her to lean against my shoulder. As the effect was so pleasant, I was glad that the position was apparently not as uncomfortable as it looked.

When we were settled, Diane asked, "Are you really sure about talking to Benzinger?"

"Yeah, I think so," I replied. "It seems like there's a couple of possibilities. One is that Jones is out to steal the technology, and getting rid of us and Benzinger pretty much clears the way for him to do whatever he wants. In that case, Benzinger's life is in danger and he should be warned."

"Yeah, I can see that," Diane said. "And the other possibility, I suppose, is that Benzinger and Jones are working together. In that case, what do we get out of this meeting?"

"We get to know who we're up against," I replied. "And we'll have a real name to give to Underwood. Sure, Benzinger will deny knowing Jones and anything about the attacks on us. But with the police knowing who he is, he'll call off his thug and we're home free."

"You know, you could handle this whole thing with a phone call." Suddenly, I wished I could see Diane's face, but in our current position, her head was nearly resting on my shoulder. Was she worried? It seemed that way.

"Maybe, but a call would be tough. Suppose he is a target. Is he going to believe me if I tell him Jones might be out to kill him? And besides, he might not even recognize my name if I call. Half the time I was there, he called me Jerry. But he'll know the face, and I'll know in 10 seconds what's going on."

Diane said nothing. I felt her move a couple of times as if she was starting to say something and then, decided to remain silent. Finally, I said, "I don't have to go."

Perhaps now, she felt the need to see my face, as she slipped her legs out and turned to look at me from the front edge of the couch. "I suppose you should ... I guess," she said with a slight frown. "I don't like it, but you're right. It's probably better face-to-face. But if you're going to do this, I'm going too. You have to admit; I was right to go with you to Frontier."

"Absolutely. No argument there. But I should go to the Science Center alone. Benzinger might be involved and there is absolutely no reason that he needs to see you there. If he does, he might connect you to this situation. And if he sees you with me, he will definitely make the connection."

"But Jones has already seen me," Diane said, the frown still on her face.

"Yeah, but he doesn't know who you are, beyond being my 'brainy, good-looking friend.' Benzinger, on the other hand ... well, you two have traveled in the same circles too long. He might take one look at you and say, 'Hey, it's

George's daughter.' Jones would be at your doorstep ten minutes after that."

Diane's frown deepened as she slowly nodded her head. "I don't recognize him, but I guess you're right."

"See, that wasn't so hard to say, was it?"

She gave me a playful punch in the arm. "Tasted like vinegar. But it's a free country, so I'm going to the Science Center. I'll keep my distance, so even if Benzinger sees me, he won't connect us. When it's over, if neither of us sees anything suspicious, we can drive home together."

She paused a moment, then said, "You also need to promise me you'll be careful."

A few tongue-in-cheek comments came to mind, but when I looked at her, none felt right. Finally, I just said, "I will, and you need to promise me the same."

She just nodded and sat there quietly, looking at me. The moments when we had laughed about our visit to Frontier, although only a few hours ago, seemed far away. Finally, she stood and said, "I'm getting a beer and after that, I'm going to bed. It might be early even after a drink, but this has been a busy day. You want a beer?"

"Sure."

She came back with two and we sat down together on the couch, each of us sipping in silence for a few minutes.

"I was just wondering," Diane said, still staring off across the room. "Why do you think Benzinger created the vest."

"So, you don't think it's a storm door?"

"Only if he has the imagination of an accountant," she said.

"Ouch, that hurt." She slid her head down along the back of the couch until it rested on my shoulder. "So, what would a brilliant doctor do with the vest?" I asked.

"Well, if nothing else, it's got to be a money machine. I mean, you could join a carnival, take it on the road, and charge a dollar a person to watch someone walk through a wall."

"Even I, the accountant, could have come up with that," I replied. "What about using it for theft? Would any vault be safe? Or military uses? You could sneak up on anyone, from any direction."

"And he could sell detection systems for it, so you'd know when the enemy was approaching. It could be like police radar detectors. The police come up with one system and a detector for it comes out. Then, the police change their radar, and we get a new detection system. It would be a cycle of technology and counter-technology until he retired a rich man."

"That might only take a few years, the way the vest would sell," I said. "But it might be tough to come up with a detection system. The vest doesn't have much range ... or at least the one we have doesn't."

"Hmm, how short?"

"Not much longer than a motorcycle," I said.

Diane poked me in the ribs. "Did you have to mention the motorcycle? I'm still trying to get that ride out of my head. But how do you know the range is six feet and not sixteen?" she asked.

"I can show you. Do you have anything about 8 to 10 feet long but light enough that we can hold it up from one end?

Something like a broom handle, except those aren't really long enough. And it can't be anything you want to keep."

"I have a curtain rod that extends that far. And it probably should have gone in the trash a long time ago."

"OK. And how about something like a board or a piece of lumber that we can push the rod through."

"There are a few old shelves in the basement," she said.

"Perfect, let's get them."

Once we had collected those items, I put on the vest and switched it on. Then, I picked up the curtain rod, about a foot from one end. "Now, hold the board up, so I can push this end of the curtain rod through it."

Diane did as I asked, and the rod went through the board easily. Then, I started sliding my hand toward the far end of the curtain rod, so that the rod stayed in place in the board while I moved backward. I reached three feet from the board, and the rod remained sticking out the other side. Then, four feet and no change. Then, five and six. But just after I passed six feet, there was a loud popping sound and a flash of light. A wisp of smoke curled into the air, smelling a bit like burnt hair.

We both gasped and I dropped my end of the curtain rod. It sheared off so that both the long end I had been holding and the six inches or so that had been sticking out beyond the board dropped to the floor. To Diane's credit, the board was still in her hands.

"Jeremy Reynolds, why didn't you warn me," she said sharply. It was a time when I would have preferred to be called honey.

"Sorry, Diane, but I had no idea. I've done something like this a couple of times and I never got anything like that. The reaction must change, depending on what material you're using. Like when the metal pole seared off in the rock on the bluffs, I never heard anything like that small explosion."

Diane, however, was just staring at the board in her hands as if she hadn't heard a word I had said. "Jeremy, look at this."

I came over to her side, looking at the spot where the curtain rod had gone through the shelf. "What is that?" I asked.

"Well, not a metal curtain rod or a board made of wood, that's for sure. It looks like getting out of the range of the vest allowed the atoms to collapse. And when they did, they formed something different than either the rod or the board."

She was quiet a moment, apparently thinking about what this discovery might mean. "I wonder if this is really why Benzinger created the device," she said. "If he could take common things, like chunks of salt or lumps of coal, and get them to combine in ways that we can't normally, maybe he could create new materials, with revolutionary properties. Materials like paper-thin, clear plastics that are as strong as sheets of steel."

"Or maybe even create things we have now, like diamonds by the handful or gold by the pound," I said. "It could be a whole new branch of chemistry, allowing scientists to create things we can only dream about or someone's personal gold mine, literally."

"Well, that would certainly be worth killing for," Diane said. "It's a sobering thought."

But when I looked at her, she seemed far away again. When she spoke, she said, "And here's another sobering thought. Give me your hand."

I wasn't sure why holding my hand would be sobering, but I didn't hesitate. "Now, step away from me as far as you can," she said. I did, while she stepped away in the other direction. "Now, what do you see?"

At first, all I saw was her, standing two arm lengths away from me. I started to say something corny, like 'a beautiful woman at the end of my arm.' And then it hit me like a punch to the stomach.

I could have killed her.

"Every time we ran, hand in hand, from Jones or his friend, you were two arm lengths away—six feet, more or less," I said. She had seen the implications even before I had, but it needed to be said. "Part of you would have been outside the field generated by the vest. If we had ever hit a fence or a wall with us that far apart, you would have lost an arm or a leg ... or worse."

I squeezed my eyes closed, forcing the image from my thoughts.

"And I know there were times when I was exhausted and was barely holding on," Diane said. "I didn't notice it at the time, but you must have always gathered me in, just as we hit something solid. That's the only way I can see that we made it. Maybe, unconsciously, you knew to keep me close."

"Maybe," I replied, but I couldn't shake my unease. "What I know consciously now, is that we can't be so careless in the future. This thing is dangerous. I'm not certain we can survive against Jones without it. But it needs to be a last resort, and preferably, one that only one of us uses at a time."

"I agree," said Diane softly. "And if we get in a tight spot, please feel free to give me a hug as we hit the next wall."

"You can count on it."

The beers we had been nursing for the last hour were gone, and I knew I was tired and perhaps a bit stressed from what we had just learned. Diane was obviously feeling the same, as she said, "I'm going up to bed, maybe read for a while, and then go to sleep."

"Yeah, I'm beat too." Feeling like we were ending the night with some considerable tension in the air, I decided to inject some humor, however feeble it might be.

"Yeah, I'm so tired, I can hardly stand," I said. And with that, I flopped down, face-first toward the floor … and disappeared.

13. A long cold one

figured that the mystery of my disappearance ended the moment I came crashing to the floor in Diane's basement. She came running down the steps.

"Jeremy, are you OK?" she called, hands waving in front of her face as she tried to clear a path through the cloud of dust I had raised.

"Yeah, not bad. Mostly embarrassed more than hurt."

She helped me untangle myself from some gardening supplies she had stored there—an old hose, a lawn sprinkler, some empty flower pots, most of which were plastic rather than terracotta clay, fortunately. A bag of potting soil had split open when I hit and was now scattered across the basement floor.

"I'll clean this up," I said.

Diane just waved her hand. "Let's get you upstairs so I can check those cuts." She was fully in doctor mode now.

After a few minutes of cleaning and bandaging, she stepped back and said, "Nothing too bad. I'd say, keep the cuts clean and change the bandages, but if you're here a few days, I'll make sure it gets done."

"Thanks, Diane ... or should I say, thanks, Doc?" I grinned at her.

"You know, as a doctor, I have plenty of business without you being a constant patient." Her gaze was unblinking as she delivered her admonition. Somehow, it felt more like the scolding a parent might give a child than the guidance of a doctor for her patient, but it was true.

"Yeah, I know. I'm not exactly the most graceful. But what surprises me, I'm really not a bad athlete. I played basketball in high school; I still play tennis. And while I'm no pro, I'm OK at both."

"Well, sports involve motor skills that you practice over and over. You get good because you hone them over time. It's possible to do sort of the same thing to improve balance in everyday life. She paused a beat. "But then, that really has nothing to do with what just happened, does it?"

"No, I guess not," I admitted. "The best balance in the world doesn't make any difference if I leave the vest turned on." But when I stopped and thought about it, that raised another question.

"Hey, Diane, something puzzles me," I said, massaging a spot on my shoulder that was still stinging from the fall. "I fell through the floor because I hit it face-first, just like walking through a wall, right? But obviously, I don't fall through the floor when I'm walking around on my feet. So, if I wasn't facing the floor, could I fall down, say on my side, and not end up in the basement?"

Diane thought a moment, her hand rubbing the back of her neck. "I'm just guessing, but it might be something like shutters. Open them the right amount, and the sunlight floods through. But open or close them more, and the light is blocked. So, you go through things you're facing, but that's it."

"You feel like trying it out?" I asked, my interest now piqued.

Diane chuckled, probably entertained by my somewhat overly-analytic nature. "Sure, why not. It'll be a while before I'll relax enough to go to sleep anyway after your vanishing act."

I turned the vest back on and we found that going through an object face-first appeared to be the only orientation that worked. Trying to slip through a wall backward or sideways was impossible. And I failed to penetrate a board that I laid on top of my head.

"Well, this explains quite a few things," I said when we were done. "I knocked Jones out with the base of that rope stand at the mall because it hit him on the side of his head. It also explains why they kept coming at us with the baseball bats. I wasn't sure how they could hurt us, but all they had to do was hit us from the side."

It felt good to take even this small step in understanding the vest, but when I glanced at Diane, it was clear she didn't share my enthusiasm. She was frowning, a wrinkle forming on her forehead, as she stared at the floor where I had disappeared.

"What's wrong?" I asked.

"Why did you stop when you hit the basement floor?"

I looked at her blankly. "Well ... maybe I twisted when I hit, got turned on my side?"

"Maybe. But I thought you were pretty much face-down in that bag of potting soil when I first saw you." Her eyes narrowed, reliving the event.

"This is easy to test," I said. "I'll just ... ah, maybe not."

"No kidding," said Diane. "You can't just go lay down on the basement floor with the vest on. I can just see you slipping out of sight. And since I can't imagine you'd come out on the other side of the earth ...." She didn't finish the thought. Didn't need to.

"But wait a minute," I said, tapping my forehead. "I've fallen down a bunch of times when I was running from Jones. I never sunk into the ground."

We were both quiet, pondering the question. Diane sat down on the couch, eyes wandering around the room. I was pacing. Finally, Diane came up with something.

"Maybe it has to do with the range of the vest. If it can penetrate the wall ... get through to the other side, you can enter. Otherwise not. What's the thickest thing you've gone through?"

"Maybe your back wall," I said, somewhat guiltily.

Diane chuckled. "You didn't even use my door?"

"I used the first wall I saw, which I might add is three or four feet above the ground outside. That hurt." Diane hid her amusement behind her hand. "But anyway, in this old house, the walls must be around a foot thick, which would fit what you said about the vest. It can penetrate that foot ... and maybe five more."

Diane nodded, looking comfortable with that conclusion. But I wasn't as certain yet. "We could check it out." She looked at me warily. "Your basement has that inside corner. I could change where I enter so that the distance through is more or less than six feet."

I thought it was a clever way to check out the vest's capabilities, but the words were hardly out of my mouth when Diane declared, "No way, Jeremy Reynolds, are you going to walk into a wall where the other side is that far away." Her lips were pressed together tightly in a line, arms folded across her chest.

"Easy, Diane," I said, meaning I understood her concern. But it must have sounded condescending as her scowl increased. I held my hands up in surrender. "No, sorry, I didn't mean I'd be walking into that wall. I have no interest in getting the angle wrong and ending up strolling around your neighborhood, ten feet below ground level."

Perhaps it was the bizarreness of the image, but her glare seemed to soften. "I just meant, I'd try sticking my arm in and pulling it back out."

She continued to frown at me for a few more moments but finally relented. After that, it only took a few moments to confirm Diane's guess. If I positioned myself so there was empty space less than six feet away, my hand entered the wall easily. But if the other side was farther away, I was blocked.

With our tests done, we went back upstairs. I found it fascinating to explore the capabilities of the vest and I knew it might save our life someday, but I'd had enough for one night.

I knew what I wanted to do, but Diane beat me to the suggestion. "Would you like to talk awhile? Maybe something besides the vest and our near-death experiences?"

"Yeah, I would."

We settled onto the couch. At first, I was slightly disappointed that she didn't tuck her legs under her and snuggle up against me as she had before, but the reason was soon clear. She sat about a foot away and brought up one leg, turning toward me. I turned to face her as well, although I left both feet on the floor.

Perhaps it was the light, but her eyes seemed more green than brown. I became lost in them as we sat there in silence.

"I have to give you credit," I said after a few minutes. "You are one cool customer. I don't know many women who could have handled that bike ride at the mall. Oh, shoot, I forgot. No talk about our near escapes. And not the bike ride in particular, right?"

She hid her laugh behind her hand, a mannerism that I was finding more and more captivating.

"Did you have braces as a kid?" I asked.

"You're talking about how I cover my mouth when I laugh? Yeah, I did. I've never been able to break the habit."

"Don't. I love it."

She looked down, blushing, her hand now just covering a smile. When she looked back at me, she said, "As for being cool under pressure, I think you're setting the bar pretty low. Yeah, I didn't throw up, but that's about all I can claim. I had my eyes shut so tight I was seeing stars. If I had any fingernails, they would have been shattered from the death grip I had on your waist. But since long fingernails don't mix with medical treatment, at least that wasn't a problem."

"Well, you fooled me. Have you always wanted to be a doctor? Sounds like you had to sacrifice your nails for the job."

"Yeah, that was a tough decision." She put her hand on her chin, eyes looking up at the ceiling as if she was pondering a particularly complex dilemma. "Nails or saving people's lives? Hmm …. Actually, for as long as I can remember, I wanted to be in medicine. My dad was a doctor, and he probably had a lot to do with my decision. And even though my mom is stay-at-home, she made it clear that medicine was as attainable as any field I might choose."

"And I take it that the private practice thing is a more recent development?" I could see her tense a bit, leaning back slightly. "I'm sorry. I've said something wrong, haven't I?"

"No, not really." She unfolded the single leg and placed her foot on the floor, but not to turn away from me. Actually, she shifted to look me directly in the face, and the phrase 'hit an issue head-on' came to my mind. "You're not asking anything that you couldn't have read about in that one news story."

I mentally kicked myself for the third time. I had never gone back to read that article. "You don't need to talk about it, if you'd rather not," I said, still feeling a little guilty about bringing up something sensitive.

"Thanks, but I have to quit hiding from what happened." She leaned forward, looking directly into my eyes. "Like I said before, I've always loved medicine, but I just about quit the field two years ago after I nearly killed a two-year-old."

"What happened?" I asked quietly.

She took a deep breath before continuing. "I was fresh out of school, and like several other times up to that point, my father had pulled some strings to get me where I was. And that was on a high-profile research program. But during one of the tests, the equipment malfunctioned and before I caught it, a two-year-old nearly died."

I reached forward, placing my hand lightly on hers. She smiled sadly, her eyes never leaving mine.

"Like I said, I almost quit then and there. Later, they found out that the only way I could have known there was a problem was if I had the equipment in diagnostic mode. And since that wasn't part of the manufacturer's written procedure, I was cleared."

She turned her hand over, lacing her fingers with mine.

"So, aren't you being a little hard on yourself by saying you nearly killed that child? You did everything right. It's a tragedy the equipment failed, but there's nothing you could have done about that."

"That's an excuse based on logic," she said. "I did everything by the book, so I did nothing wrong. But it doesn't help. I keep wondering if a more experienced doctor would have caught it. Anyway, I haven't set foot in the lab since. And I never will."

Everything she had said had been delivered calmly, but with perhaps a trace of sadness. But with the last statement, an edge appeared in her tone. She had made up her mind, and I felt her hand tighten around mine.

"And the clinic where you are now? It's the way back to the career you love?"

"Exactly," she said and the tension was broken, a slight smile reaching her lips. "I'm good with patients."

"I can attest to that," I said. Her smile broadened.

"Thanks," she said. "I can't escape death. It's part of the job. But if I have to face it, I want it to be when I'm helping people, not testing some new drug. I know that research is necessary, vital really. But it's just not my thing."

"How'd you get into it then? Or was that what you meant when you said something about your dad pulling strings?" I asked. But as I spoke, I realized how one-sided this conversation had become, with me asking personal questions and her baring her soul. I had the sense that she wanted to tell me, that she felt good about discussing her life, but I wasn't certain.

"I'm sorry," I said. "This is beginning to sound like the Inquisition. Am I being too nosy?"

"No, not at all," she said quickly. She released my hand and raised hers to lightly touch my chest. It was a gesture that I didn't quite understand, but the contact made me shiver. "I like talking to you. As for my dad, yeah, he loves research and wanted me to share that passion. But it's just not in my DNA. He had a lot to do with my love of medicine, just not his particular brand of it."

Diane dropped her hand back to where it laid on mine and leaned back on the couch. She stretched and yawned.

"Getting sleepy?" I asked.

"Yeah, a bit. But can we talk a few more minutes?"

"Of course. All night if you want."

"I'd never last that long." She paused, looking at me. "I just wonder why it is that I find you so easy to talk to? I'm sitting here, spilling my guts about things that I've hardly mentioned to anyone else."

"Just a sympathetic face," I replied.

"A nice face, but that's not it," she said. That bit of flattery caused an instant spike in my ego, although the possibility that this was all just a build-up before teasing me crossed my mind as well. I figured it was a win either way.

Finally, she said, "I think it's because I can tell you exactly what's on my mind. No offense to the fair-haired of my gender, but I could never see playing the dumb blonde.

I'm a brunette, after all. But if I say what's on my mind to a lot of guys, they don't stick around."

"You just need to find a guy running for his life. He'll stick around. In fact, you could have a hard time getting rid of him," I said. She chuckled. "But seriously, any guy who didn't stick around for you must be blind."

"You're sweet, Jeremy, but I didn't mean looks. If I say something about chemistry, or physiology, or medicine, they look at me as if I'm speaking a foreign language. But you don't seem to mind. In fact, you often start it, what with all those anomalous thrust devices or whatever they were."

"Yeah, I was raised with all that brainy talk. Did I mention that my parents were both university faculty?"

"Really?" she said. She sat up a little straighter on the couch, looking into my eyes.

"Yep, the same department even—astronomy."

"That's why you knew about space-travel research?"

"Yeah, I'm undoubtedly more curious about that kind of thing than the average person," I admitted.

"So, how'd it work with both parents in the same academic department?"

"Only way it could. My dad was a well-respected member of the faculty. My mom was the department chair, his boss."

I had coaxed a few smiles out of Diane along the course of our talk, perhaps even a chuckle or two, but this was the first real laugh, complete with her hand shielding her mouth. I could feel the warmth of her laughter washing over me.

"Actually, I think it would have worked the other way, too. My mom and dad were opposites, but they knew it and embraced it rather than trying to fix it. Their favorite saying was, 'What do you expect? Opposites attract.' I always thought at the level of basic values—what's really important in life—they had a lot in common. But on everyday things, not so much. If they went to the movies and my mom wanted to see a comedy, he would be in the mood for action-adventure."

"And us?" Diane asked. "Are we opposites?"

Us?

I wasn't expecting that question. I didn't know Diane even thought that there was an us, let alone whether we agreed or not. But then again, it's just small talk.

"I don't know. But I'm certain you're female and I'm male. That's about as opposite as it gets."

Diane shook her head in mock disgust at my comment. "Spoken just like a man. Take a simple question and turn it into a matter of sex." Her hand came back to my chest, this time giving me a little push. But she leaned forward as she did, so that our faces ended up closer than they had been, a playful smile on her lips, a twinkle in her eyes.

The conversation had relaxed me, but it was much more than that. The smooth, soft lines of her body, sitting there on the couch in front of me; her smell; the hazel pools of her eyes; the sensual curve of her lips when she smiled; the quiet laughs she hid behind her hand—it was an intoxicating mix that I couldn't resist. I leaned toward her, looking into her eyes, hoping she felt as I did.

But if she did, she completely missed my overture.

"This will never do," she said, suddenly standing and walking to a chair on the other side of the room where I had laid the vest. She walked back toward me, then turned and circled around the back of the couch. "Here. I can make something like a clothes valet. It'll let you keep the vest close, just in case."

"Yeah, never hurts to be prepared," I said, wondering what had just happened. Maybe she had glanced away, just as I had drawn close to her?

She had dropped the vest on a different chair and was now mindlessly rubbing one hand up and down her arm, pacing around the room. The sudden spike in nervous energy was making me uneasy and I said, "Do you want to sit down, maybe talk for a few more minutes?"

"Oh, you know, I'm pretty tired. Maybe I'll just head up to bed."

She turned and headed for the stairs while I just sat there, a blank look on my face. When she reached the foot of the stairs, she turned and said, "Jeremy, I'm glad you're here. I'll sleep better just knowing it."

"I'm glad I'm here, too," I replied.

She nodded and left. But as she disappeared up the stairs, I wondered if sleep would come at all. My senses were filled with her presence; my mind's eye saw only her. Finally, I decided to go to one of the first places I had ever discovered in her home—the downstairs bathroom. I took a long, cold shower and went to bed.

14. Dodging cars and killers

When I awoke on Sunday morning after sleeping what could not have been more than four hours, I went into the kitchen and started the coffee. Then, I checked the cabinets and the refrigerator. I figured it wasn't snooping; it was earning my keep. It wasn't long until I heard Diane's step on the stairs.

"Good morning," I said, as she came down. She was wearing the same gym shorts and T-shirt ensemble. I tried not to stare. "Coffee?" I asked.

"Yes, please. As strong as yesterday, I hope."

"Only way to make it." And I poured her a cup.

"What's that you're mixing up in the bowl?" she asked.

"I took a chance you'd be in the mood for pancakes."

"I love pancakes, but honey, you don't need to cook every morning."

Honey?

I missed a beat again when she reverted to her pet name for me. But given her reaction last night, maybe she used that shorthand for a lot of people. I set the thought aside, responding to my stomach instead.

"Actually, I do have to cook, unless you want to eat cereal. I checked your cabinets. Do you really eat that chocolate puffed stuff?"

"Hey, no one in my presence is allowed to say anything negative about chocolate in any form, at any time of day. And yeah, sometimes I grab a bowl of it in the morning. I have some really early morning starts. But then again, you know all about that, don't you?" She cocked an eyebrow and flashed me a lewd smile.

Even though she was just teasing, I couldn't fully hide my embarrassment. "You're never going to let me forget that, are you?" I asked, slowly shaking my head.

"Never ... unless you finally stop blushing every time I ask." She laughed so softly that I only knew she was from the movement of her shoulders. "So, Sunday morning is my time to re-stock at the grocery store. You want something besides the chocolate, puffed cereal. Good. You come along and pick it out."

"I can do that," I said, as I ladled pancake batter onto the hot griddle.

"Great. Since you're already dressed, I'll go get changed. Back in a few for breakfast." Diane headed upstairs.

When she returned, I said, "I don't have enough room to make more than a short stack at a time, so you need to eat yours while they're hot. I'll join you as soon as the second batch is done."

She sat down in front of the plate and took a bite. "Mmm. These are delicious. Is everything you cook as good as the omelet and these pancakes?"

"I only know how to cook a few things, and most of them are comfort food—fried chicken, meatloaf, just about anything barbequed, a few breakfasts. I'll start a grocery list while these last pancakes finish cooking."

"I'm mostly a 'wing it' kind of shopper, but that sounds good," said Diane.

"How about beef stew? Mine's not bad, especially since the weather's getting colder. A bowl of that and a biscuit will warm you up."

"Sure, that sounds good. But isn't that a bit ... involved."

"You have one of those slow cookers?" Diane nodded. "Then, there's nothing to it." I wrote down what I needed, then asked, "You like fried chicken? It's my specialty."

"Umm, OK. But that's a couple of pretty heavy meals. You need to back off a bit."

"OK. How about chicken burritos? I grill skinless breasts, so that's about as light as you can get. And you can pick and choose the other ingredients—shredded cheese, avocado, black beans, sour cream. Or you can just put a couple of sprigs of lettuce on yours, and I'll eat all the good stuff."

Diane was snickering behind her hand. "OK, put burritos on the list, but you're done. I'll have shin splints by the time I jog off those three meals."

The pancakes were done so I piled them on the serving plate. "Better have some more because it sounds like it's going be chocolate puffed cereal for the rest of the week."

Diane got up from her chair, grabbed me by the shoulders, guided me to my seat at the island, and pushed me down. "Those are all yours," she said, grinning. "And give me that grocery list. It's going to be salads for the rest of the week."

After chuckling under my breath for a moment and taking a couple of bites of breakfast, I ventured a thought. "So, you asked me last night about whether we had any differences? I think we just hit the mother lode."

Diane pretended to ignore me, although I could see the corner of her mouth turn up. "I like a lot of different toppings on salads," she said after a moment. "I'll list what I usually get and you can add what you want afterward. Let's see, tomatoes, carrots, black olives, red and green peppers ...."

I lost track after she hit twenty different toppings. When she finished, she asked, "Anything you want to add?"

"How about a grilled pork chop smothered in gravy?"

She rolled her eyes. "I'll take that as a no. Now, if you haven't eaten so many pancakes that you can't get out of the chair, let's go to the store."

As she passed me on the way to retrieve her jacket for the trip, she paused at my chair, bent down, kissed me on the cheek. She left the kitchen without a word.

What just happened?

I thought about calling her back, but I couldn't find my voice. I just sat there for what seemed only a few moments, wondering if I understood her at all when I heard the front door open. She was going out to her car. I jumped up and ran to follow.

△ △ △

Shopping was almost as entertaining as putting the list together, but we were soon back at her place and put the food away. We had bought a couple of deli sandwiches and we had them for lunch. Then, I volunteered to clear the table, while she went to get ready for our visit to the Science Center.

When that was done, there were still a few toiletries we had purchased setting on the counter. I carried them upstairs, then called down the hall before proceeding. I'd lose what little credibility I had earned if I walked in on her in a state of undress again.

"In here," she said, and I entered her bedroom. She was apparently thinking about what to wear as her closet door was open and she was flipping through the dresses hanging there.

"Oh, thanks, Jeremy," she said when she turned around. "Just toss that stuff on the bed. I'll put it away later."

When she went back to the dresses, her hand went past a short, red one with a somewhat low neckline. I couldn't help but think how stunning she would look in it with her fair complexion and dark brown hair. No male in attendance would be able to take his eyes off her. Fortunately, she had more sense than me and pulled out a simple gray dress, much more consistent with keeping a low profile.

I went back downstairs and consulted my limited wardrobe—would it be this pair of jeans or the other one? But I had a pair of khaki pants in the drawer somewhere and after some digging, I found them and a polo shirt. I grabbed an umbrella, too, as it looked a bit like rain. I was just coming back into the living room after getting dressed as Diane was coming down the stairs. Yes, the gray dress was more conservative, but I still couldn't resist stealing glances at her legs and the smooth curves of her body. I wasn't sure it was possible for Diane to be inconspicuous.

We sat on the couch and formulated our plan for confronting Benzinger. We decided to take her car since Jones might recognize mine if he was there. We'd park it in Forest Park, near the J.S. McDonnell Planetarium. The Planetarium was north of Interstate 64, while the Science Center was directly south, on the other side of the freeway. To go between them, I had two options. There was a pedestrian walkway—a skybridge as they called it—from the main Science Center building over I-64 to a small entry structure on the other side. The Planetarium was just a short distance to the north along a footpath. The other option was a less-traveled, pedestrian tunnel under I-64.

After confronting Benzinger, whether he seemed a threat or not, the plan was for me to leave him and then, double back along my path. That way, I hoped to spot anyone following me. I would return to the car at exactly 3:30 using either the skybridge or the tunnel, whichever seemed safer. Diane would stay hidden in the parking lot, watching to make sure I was alone before she joined me for the drive back.

It all sounded good ... on paper.

Several times during the ride over, Diane reminded me of my promise to be careful. For my part, of course, I had no intention of doing anything risky. It was to be a quick talk and an even faster retreat. And after that, we could consider next steps at our leisure and in the safety of her home.

"There's a coffee shop, just over on the other side of I-64 on Oakland," I said as she parked her car. "It's a long time until I'll be back here." It was only about 1:45.

"I think I might be a little too nervous to be sipping coffee. I'll just mill around in the crowds, keep my eyes open for Jones."

"Sure, but like we talked about, hang back in the corners, wherever you are out of sight. You don't want Jones seeing you before you see him. I'm not the only one taking a chance here. You need to be careful, too."

I reached across the seat and took her hand. She looked down at our hands, then back up at me, smiling. "I'll be careful."

I exited the car. She would be following a few minutes later. As soon as I reached the skybridge, I joined the crowd flowing toward the Center. The panel discussion had drawn a decent group for a Sunday afternoon talk, and I knew I would have little trouble blending in.

I found Boeing Hall easily, the location for the panel discussion. As I might have expected from aerospace-giant Boeing, the hall had the feel of an aircraft hangar with an arched roof and exposed metal beams throughout. The area had been divided into seating for the presentation on one side, fronted by a raised platform for the panel. The other side of the room held sparsely place tables where the reception would be held.

I took a seat and soon, the introductions began. If there was any lingering doubt hidden in the depths of my mind, it disappeared as the person I knew as Johannes Schmidt stepped on the stage second and was introduced as Dr. Nils Benzinger. As I sat there listening I had to admit, he had a presence, a way about him that made me want to believe he wasn't involved with Jones. But public personas were what people wanted them to be, and I knew it was more likely than not that he and Jones were working together.

The hour for the panel discussion went quickly. Under different circumstances, I probably would have been absorbed by some of the concepts that were being discussed.

But questions of Benzinger's honesty kept stealing my attention.

The reception that followed was informal with a few dozen people milling around with the presenters, offering their viewpoints and expressing their appreciation. I approached Benzinger from behind and heard him say, "Yes, I get out on the Great River Trail South just about every day over lunch for a run."

I was surprised. He looked like he rarely got up from his desk, let alone went jogging. But then, 10 minutes at four miles an hour might be what he considered a run for all I knew.

"Thank you, Dr. Benzinger, for sharing your perspective. It was quite inspiring," said his current fan, a woman whose gray hair nearly matched her suit. She and her friends moved away, leaving Benzinger alone. It was my opportunity.

"Dr. Benzinger," I said. "Or should I say, Dr. Schmidt?"

I thought there was a slight hitch in his movement, but his face was blank by the time he had completed the turn to face me.

"I don't believe we've had the pleasure," he said. "I'm Nils Benzinger. I'm not familiar with anyone named .... What did you say, Schmidt?"

"My mistake. You can call me Jones." If he wasn't going to be straight with me, I thought I'd reply in kind. "Thomas Jones."

"Wouldn't that be a fairly common American name? Didn't you even have a singer named Tom Jones?"

"He's Welsh, actually." I wasn't certain just where I had picked up that bit of trivia, but since it was something I could throw in his face, I was glad I knew it.

Walking away at that point would have been the intelligent thing to do. The fact that he pretended not to know me or recognize the name was all the proof I really needed. Benzinger was involved in this thing—whatever it was—right up to his gray, bushy eyebrows. But something about someone wanting to kill me was fueling my temper, and I wanted to see if I could make him a bit uncomfortable. He'd certainly done no less to Diane and me.

"Your talk was nice, Dr. B, but I was really hoping you would speak about your research on weatherproofing homes. Or maybe, just walking through walls?"

He tilted his head to one side and stuck his hands in his suit coat pockets. Then, slowly, he said, "I think you're mistaken, both about what I've done and the laws of physics. Now, if you'll excuse me." He turned to leave. Again, following his example was the smart choice, but I couldn't just yet.

"I'm wearing the vest," I said, just loud enough for him to hear.

Benzinger turned around and looked at my clothes. I tugged at the bottom of my shirt, so the outline of the vest would be visible. Then, he shrugged and waved a hand at me, as if I was a bothersome insect. "I'm not certain what your cheap attire has to do with me."

"Perhaps I should turn it on, give everyone in this room a demonstration. Say, walk through that partition over there," I said, nodding with my head.

Benzinger stared at me a moment. Finally, he said, "You're obviously delusional. But let's say, for the sake of discussion, that you could, as you put it, walk through that partition. What then? Well, I suspect that since you are so obviously unqualified to have created the technology required for such a feat, the real developer will step forward, complete with plans and maybe even patent applications? And then the question becomes, how is it in your possession?"

"There might be some question about what I've done, but in the end, I'll bring you down." I gritted my teeth, fists forming at my side.

Benzinger laughed. "Ah, Mr. Jones, was it? Just what is it that you think I've done? If I had invented anything like what you describe, I would go to great lengths to protect it. I'd keep it hidden from the public, under false names and fake businesses. After all, it's a competitive world out there. But the thing is, there's nothing illegal about that. Nothing at all. In fact, it's almost standard practice. But then, with your obvious background in what? Temp labor? I guess you wouldn't know anything about that."

I could feel my fingernails biting into the palms of my hands, my heart rate climbing. He was pushing all my buttons. "Hiring some goon to kill me isn't legal."

"You mean, this hypothetical developer of a device that violates the laws of physics? He hired someone to kill you? You really should go to the police with that. I can't imagine the outrage they'd feel, knowing that such a fine, marginal representative of society had been threatened."

I pushed my anger down, focusing on his words. His taunt was virtually the same as one Jones had used—that no one would care about a crime against me, because I was ... no one. I hadn't picked the job with Schmidt and Jones; they had picked me.

"Oh, Mr. Jones, just one other story before I must take my leave. Some years ago, an academic—let's call him Dr. X—leaked a story about another professor's work. Dr. X didn't steal the work; he just told the public what was coming. The second man did nothing about it. But then, after a few years had passed, the second man planted falsified data in Dr. X's research. The fake data was discovered and Dr. X was discredited, losing his job and then, his wife. He ended up killing himself."

I shook my head, holding my hands out, palms up. "I don't get it. What's this got to do with you and your vest?"

"There was no money involved, just reputation. And yet, the second man went to great lengths to exact the ultimate vengeance on Dr. X. Imagine what your hypothetical developer will do to you if you rob him of his just rewards." He turned and started walking away, his threat hanging in the air.

When he was about 10 feet away, he turned back. "You know," he said, in a mockingly pleasant tone, "it's amazing what you can learn to do on your smartphone just using your sense of touch. It seems that I've sent a text message a full five minutes ago." He pulled his phone from his jacket pocket.

It was clear that Benzinger had prepared for a possible confrontation. And like every other encounter, he and Jones were ahead of me. Now the only question was, how far ahead? Had he done more than just think about how to handle my threats? Did he have Jones lurking in the shadows or on the way? I thought about smashing my umbrella into his smug face, but that would only produce a moment's satisfaction. I turned to leave.

Clearly, all I had accomplished after the first 10 seconds of our talk was to give him the opportunity to call Jones. It was time to retreat; hopefully, I had not already delayed too long. Five minutes by itself meant little without knowing where Jones was. But it was five minutes and counting.

I exited the main entrance to the Science Center and headed for the parking lot behind. That lot would be the default choice for anyone going to the talk. If Benzinger was watching me, hopefully, he would send Jones that way. Then, doubling back, I watched for Jones or Benzinger as I returned to the Center.

Suddenly, up ahead in a group walking toward me, I spotted Jones. Diving behind a potted plant, I landed hard. The knee of my pants ripped and blood began oozing from a wound.

"Young man, are you hurt?" It was an elderly lady with blue hair, hovering about five feet away. She probably thought that was close enough, thinking my irrational behavior might return at any moment.

"I'm OK," I replied, smiling, hoping she would just walk away.

"Oh, goodness, you're bleeding. I'm going to get help." And without another word, she turned and scurried off.

Between my nose-dive and the well-intentioned old lady, half the people in the Center's entrance hall were now staring at me. I looked around to see where Jones had gone. First, I spotted some other members of the group he had been in. And then, I saw him, but it wasn't Jones. It was just someone that looked a lot like him. I guessed that Underwood was right. There were a lot of people that fit his description.

I got up, my knee hurting from the abuse I had dealt it. The rip and the growing, bloody spot on my pants were going to make being discreet an impossibility, so speed became a more important tactic. I rushed off, deeper into the Science Center.

In a few minutes, I had made my way to the skybridge without further sightings of Jones, real or imagined. But the bridge was much busier than expected. It wasn't just the audience from the panel discussion, but rather an influx of parents and kids who were enjoying the exhibits. All the blind spots behind displays where Jones might be lurking was a problem, but the milling crowd made it even worse. I could see myself hustling over the skybridge, only to have a concerned parent call security because there was a bloody man running among the kids.

So, I doubled back again, leaving the Center by the main entrance and walking along Oakland Avenue toward the pedestrian tunnel. It was much quieter on the street with only a few people, mostly couples or small groups, strolling along. Perhaps this time, all would go smoothly. And it was until I heard the sound of running feet approaching from behind. I turned my vest on.

Unless I can ....

I turned the vest off and drew my umbrella back, intending to take a vicious swing at my oncoming assailant. If I waited to the last second, my swing should catch Jones on the side of his head. Hitting him at that spot, even if his vest was on, might stop him. If I missed and struck him in the face, then the worst that would happen is that my umbrella, as well as my arm and maybe all of me, would pass right through. And if he hadn't bothered to turn on his vest? Well, then any type of strike would work. It was worth a try.

Just as the footsteps arrived at my back, I spun around as forcefully as I could with my arm flying forward like I was cracking a whip. Or I would have if my umbrella hadn't snagged on the back of my jacket. As it was, I nearly tore my arm out of its socket, with all the unreleased torque it took.

Normally, I would have been furious with my lack of coordination. It was, after all, the story of my life—falling from shelves, running into doors, having my feet fly out from under me. But in this case, I was never happier to be a klutz. Because there, standing in front of me, her hands on her knees as she gasped for breath, was Diane.

"What are you doing here?" I managed to ask, staring in disbelief. "I thought you'd be watching from the other side of the freeway?"

"What happened to you?" she asked between gasps for air as she looked at my knee. Her face was flushed with the exertion, a sheen of sweat on her lip.

"A disagreement with the floor," I replied. "I'll tell you later. We need to get moving because Benzinger texted Jones. He's on the way."

"No," she said. "He's here. He's on the other side of the tunnel waiting for you with a gun. We need to go back to the skybridge."

"A gun?" Diane nodded, still catching her breath. I gaped at the tunnel's entrance only about three feet away. If I had entered it, Jones could have opened fire at any time. It wasn't like there was anywhere to run. And all I had to do was flinch, turn away, and I'd be dead.

"OK," I said, "but I'm going to cause a scene, going back through the Center like this."

Diane reached in her pocket and pulled out a scarf. "Here, tie this around your knee."

"It'll get ruined," I said. She gave me one of those 'you have to be kidding looks.' I took the scarf and did as I was told.

"There," she said. "That'll probably start a new fashion trend. Let's go."

We snuck back into the Center and spent the longest 35 minutes of my life making our way across the skybridge. We did something like 'leap-frog.' First, I went forward, found a spot and hid behind a display or in the door of an open room. Then, Diane moved, taking a position beyond me. It was slow, but at least one of us always had the other's back. And after it was over, we had seen no one.

We finally reached her car and drove back to her house. One of her neighbors was evidently having some type of party—perhaps an early Thanksgiving celebration—and she had to park a block away.

By the time we walked to her house, it was 7:00 o'clock and we were both hungry. While we had bought ingredients for several home-cooked meals and all kinds of salads, Diane suggested we have a frozen pizza. I had convinced her that an emergency meal when we were both too tired to cook was in order. But I don't think either of us had expected to be having it this soon.

While it was cooking, Diane cleaned and bandaged another of my wounds. It was getting to be a well-practiced routine for the two of us. After the pizza was done, I grabbed a couple of beers so we could unwind. We took a seat on the couch, and I recounted my discussion with Benzinger.

"That's about it," I said, as I finished my story. Diane had sat quietly throughout the telling, mostly staring at the floor, picking at her pizza.

Now she looked up, chewing on her bottom lip. "I think you're right. He was expecting you. His answers were all too good, too quick, too pat. If we do nothing, Jones eventually hunts us down. But if we do something to expose him or his technology—take his name to the police, demonstrate the vest to reporters at the St. Louis Post Dispatch, whatever. Maybe he gets egg on his face for some excessive business practices, but he keeps the vest, gets rich, and eventually, he gets even."

I took a long pull on my beer, wondering if there was a more positive spin I could put on our situation. I failed to come up with anything. "That would be my interpretation of that strange story about the two professors as well. But if we can make the connection between Jones and Benzinger, he goes to jail and loses the technology. No tech, no money, and we're safe. Or at least, safer."

Diane took a deep breath and let it out, but said nothing. A few minutes later, the cycle repeated. I let her think in silence. Finally, she turned to me on the couch and said, "Can we do this? Make the connection between them?"

I took both of her hands in mine. "Benzinger's got some criminal purpose for the vest. He's not going to call Jones off, and I don't want to wait for that goon to succeed. We've got to try."

"Well, they don't know who I am, so you're safe here until we can figure out a way to expose them."

"Right," I replied. "Once we figure out the trap, I lure them in and you bring in the police."

She sighed again, looking at me for the longest time. Then, she simply said, "OK."

We both leaned back on the couch in silence. After a while, I picked up my beer for the last swallow.

"I'm glad to see you're getting that to your mouth so easily." I turned to her, frowning in my confusion. "I mean, I'm glad your shoulder can take the strain."

I winced, realizing the ribbing that was coming. But in the current situation, it was a welcome diversion. "Were my intentions that obvious?"

"You nearly spun out of your shoes when your umbrella got snagged," she said smiling. Then, turning more serious, she took both of my hands in hers and said, "But today, that little motor-skill disconnect of yours probably saved me a lot of pain."

"Motor-skill disconnect? Is that the politically correct term for a total klutz?" I asked.

"Naw, just professional doctor talk." I rolled my eyes as dramatically as I could.

"I would have called out to warn you, but I was so out of breath from running. I had to catch you before you got to the tunnel."

"You saved my life." She smiled at me, sad and happy at the same time. "I'm just glad you got across the skybridge fast enough to warn me. It was crowded."

Diane was quiet, and I started thinking she was letting me off easy. There was lots of fodder for teasing me in that clumsy maneuver. And then, almost under her breath, she said, "I didn't exactly go that way."

I turned toward her and waited, but it didn't appear that she was going to volunteer anything more. "So, where'd you come from?"

"That's not important," she said, waving a hand, which of course, made it vital information to me.

"No, seriously. How'd you get there? If you went in disguise through the tunnel, that's a bit dicey, but I could see it." I waited.

"I ran across I-64," she said, in the same tone she might have used to tell me she bought some new shoelaces.

"You did what?" I said. I ran my hand through my hair and slid forward on the couch so I could look into her eyes. "One of the busiest roads in the city, and you decide to run across it in the middle of the day? What is it there? Six or eight lanes?"

"I lost count. And besides, it's Sunday," she said, shrugging as if that explained her action.

What are you going to do? Yell at the woman who risked her life because you were about to walk into a trap? Not say anything and imply that it was OK with you? The logic of any statement was escaping me. Finally, I just said, "I guess we need a little better understanding of what the phrase 'be careful' means."

"Yes, Jeremy," she said in one of those voices you might hear a toddler use when scolded by a parent and the child wanted to appear apologetic while feeling anything but sorry. I could only shake my head in submission.

I picked up the empties and carried them into the kitchen, disposing of them in the recycling container. "Want anything else to drink?" I called through the kitchen door. I heard a 'no' and returned to Diane and the couch empty-handed. She had resumed that legs-tucked-under, sitting position that looked painful, if not impossible, and was twirling a strand of her hair around a finger. I sat down beside her and she snuggled up to me.

I didn't want to talk any more about Benzinger, Jones, or how to defeat them. We'd have plenty of time to consider our state and the way out in the next few days, and Diane's unfocused gaze told me that she probably felt the same. But the vest technology itself? Well, that was a different story in my mind.

"Any interest in combining a few other things with the vest? Who knows, we could come up with the formula for diamonds. And the fireworks might be fun."

Diane pulled back far enough to look at me, her face scrunched up. "Why is it that all guys like to blow things up?" she asked.

I shrugged and said, "Why is it that women don't?"

Diane shook her head as if resigned to the opposite sex's attachment to pyrotechnics. "That curtain rod made quite a pop, and it was only about an inch around. I don't think I'd be comfortable throwing handfuls of random stuff together. Yeah, we might stumble across something interesting, or we might blow ourselves up."

"It just seems a waste to leave this incredible piece of technology sitting around," I said. "But I can see your point."

Diane resettled herself into her position snuggled against my chest. That alone was enough to discourage any more wild ideas from me. We sat in silence for a few more minutes. The stress of the day, coupled with the lack of sleep the previous night, started to overtake me and I yawned. It was contagious.

Diane stretched, uncoiling her lithe body on the couch beside me. It was impossible for me to look away. Her sweater rode up as she raised her hands above her head, working the kinks in her shoulders and neck. My mind was filled with the thought of reaching out and touching the soft skin that was exposed. I hadn't really planned on renewing my overtures, reasoning that rejections two days in a row might be difficult to swallow. And while the pretend fights over meals had been fun, overall, the day had been taxing. Certainly, nothing had happened that suggested we were closer. Arguing with a deranged genius and dodging cars on a busy freeway had left us no time to develop a deeper chemistry.

But even with no reason to believe that anything had changed, I had no power to resist her. I decided to shift the conversation to anything more personal than the piece of tech that had dominated our lives recently. But I was too late.

"This is embarrassing because it's so early, but I didn't sleep that well last night," Diane said, pushing herself upright beside me, a tired smile on her face. "I'm going to go up and maybe read for a while, then go to bed. Jeremy, thanks for being a friend." She lightly laid a hand on my arm as she rose from the couch. Even with the disappointment of this turn of events, that gesture was enough to raise goosebumps on my skin.

"Of course," I said. "We'll get through this."

After she left, I sat on the couch, thinking about what she had said. Being just a friend, long term, would be difficult for me to accept. Even now, it was driving me crazy. But a man who had been slowly sinking into obscurity probably had little to offer a woman who was taking her life back, making a niche for herself in a demanding career she loved.

I was about to head to the bathroom for another cold shower when a creak on the stairs made me look over. Diane was now in her shorts and T–shirt ensemble. She walked over without saying a word, stopping mere inches away. Warmth radiated from her body. Her smell filled my senses. Slowly, she drew her fingertips across my chest, leaving a tingling sensation in their wake. I slipped one hand behind her neck and bent down. She leaned in to meet me. We kissed, long, and slow, and deep. As she pulled back, a smile curled her lips.

"Would you like to come upstairs?" she asked.

"Very much."

15. A Norvell Rockwell picture

The lack of warmth of Diane's body nestled against my back, her arm no longer wrapped across my shoulder woke me. Instead, she was sitting up beside me, staring at the door.

"Is there something wrong?" I asked, stretching and rubbing the sleep from my eyes.

"I'm not sure. I thought I heard something a few minutes ago. I'm not positive I was even awake. And I haven't heard anything since."

Alarms started going off in my head. That was more than enough to jar me fully awake. "I think I better check it out."

We both dressed silently and I slipped on the vest, hitting the power switch. Having our first and best line of defense available was prudent if this proved to be more than the creaking floor of an old home or the sounds of a squirrel running across the roof.

Suddenly, Jones stepped through the closed bedroom door, gun in hand. My heart went into overdrive, as I realized that Diane was far outside the range of the vest. My eyes went to her face, but she was glaring at Jones.

"Ah, what a lovely, domestic picture this is," said Jones. "Fit for a Norvell Rockwell picture, it is." I was certain he meant Norman Rockwell but decided not to correct him. No reason to start off being argumentative. I was sure that would come later.

"Take up housekeeping with your brainy friend, did you, Jeremy ol' boy? Or should I say, Dr. Diane Stapleton? Easy on the eyes, this one. And a bit of a celebrity too. Well, doctors who almost kill their patients do make the news."

"I wouldn't have bothered to save the patient if it had been you," she spat at him, her face flushed with anger.

Jones appeared the formidable foe, as his muscles rippled in what might have been the same black T-shirt he had worn before. But together, we outnumbered and outweighed him. If I could get Diane within the protective field of my vest, she would be safe from his gun. That was, I corrected myself, as long as I faced Jones. One turn to the side and we'd be dead.

But then, if we waded into a direct attack on him, how would that work? Anything straight in front of me would be nothing more than thin air, but the same would be true of anything Jones faced. Could Diane and I adjust our assault quickly enough to ever strike a blow, as we spun and fought for position? Or would I see my fist pass through Jones, only to watch it land on the side of Diane's head?

In a world without vests, I liked our chances against Jones, but that wasn't the reality of our situation. I needed to think. There had to be another option.

"So, let's get this over with," said Jones, baring his teeth. "Why don't you slip off that vest and we can go for a little ride. Make it easy for me, and I'll make it easy for you. But you give me any trouble, and I'll let you watch while I make your little doctor friend suffer. Might even have some fun with her. And then, it'll be your turn to die."

My blood pressure soared with the direct threat to Diane and I took a step forward, unable to contain myself. But Jones's pistol snapped up, not pointing at my head, but at Diane's. I forced my feet to a stop, the adrenaline coursing through my bloodstream.

"Got a little soft spot there for the young Miss Pretty, don't you, Jeremy ol' boy?"

I closed my eyes for a moment, trying to clear my head of the rage that reigned there. There was nothing to gain from a blind attack and everything to lose. I glanced at Diane again, but she was still glowering at Jones.

"What was that look?" asked Jones. His voice was cold, his stare, flinty. "You're not thinking of doing something stupid, are you, Jeremy? You see, I really don't want to shoot you here. It would make too much of a mess. But frankly, I'm tired of the games, so here and now or later? It's your choice, but make it fast."

I had no plan, no idea how we might overcome him. This wasn't like the storeroom, where there had been space to maneuver. And the vastness of the backyards of south St. Louis seemed limitless compared to Diane's tiny bedroom. The only option I could see, for what it was worth, was to keep him talking and hope that he would make a mistake or something would come to us. At least that ploy was within reach, as he obviously liked the sound of his own voice.

"We went to the police with Schmidt's real identity," I said. "You'd be doing yourself a favor if you cut your losses and get out of here."

"I don't think so," Jones said, smirking. "If you were going to out Benzinger, you would have done it at the Science Center. But showing the vest to the world hurts you a lot more than him. He still walks; he still ends up with enough money to bury you and your brainy friend. I don't think he left you any options."

"You don't think he left me options," I said, derisively. "Or is that what Benzinger told you to think?"

I wondered for a second if he understood me because there seemed to be little reaction. And then, he turned red with rage, nostrils flaring as he worked the muscles in his jaw. Had I pushed him too far? Would he just shoot Diane and then deal with me? I had to be careful that we didn't cross that line because escaping without her wasn't an option. It was going to be both of us or I wasn't going anywhere.

"I think for myself," he boomed, a vein bulging in his forehead. "Yeah, Benzinger's a genius, obviously. He's ten times the two of you put together. But he's in my pocket. He's book-smart, but he doesn't know the street. He'd never cross me because then he'd have to find someone else to take care of all the little, dirty details. He'd be right back where he is now, but with me to deal with as well."

Keep talking.

"I agree," I said mildly, hoping to lower the temperature of this discussion because it was about to boil over. "He hasn't got the guts to deal with you now. But soon, your usefulness is over. And when that happens, there'll be a little accident in his lab and you'll find your atoms merged with a pile of cow manure. That doesn't take any guts at all. It just takes a deceitful mind, and Benzinger's well qualified for that."

I had obviously misjudged what it took to calm him, as he roared, "Shut the hell up." His T-shirt appeared to be on the verge of ripping, as every muscle in his body tensed. "And take the damn vest off."

I had pushed him so far that there was no option other than to comply. But as my hand raised to the first button, Diane spoke.

"By the way, I'm sorry you had to die out on Billingsley Road after the mall," she said.

It was a brilliant opening and a rush of relief spread over me, as her words made it clear she was joining the stalling effort. Jones sneered. He evidently found something amusing in Diane's words, giving us a few more precious moments to come up with a plan. I needed them because I still had no clue what we could do.

"Yeah, that was brilliant, wasn't it?" Jones said, smirking. "Giving myself Tom's name. Benzinger just said, pick a common American name. Using Tom Jones was all my idea."

"Tom Jones the singer is Welsh, you know," I added, hoping it was fodder for discussion and not a reason for him to pull the trigger.

"I said to shut up," bellowed Jones, again focusing his icy glare on me. No one seemed to care about this bit of trivia, but I did learn that he was near his breaking point with me. I was able to take a breath when Diane rejoined the delaying tactic.

"But you must have been sad to see your friend die," she said. I only hoped she was thinking about escape tactics as well as stalling maneuvers.

Jones broke out in a fit of laughter, slapping his free hand on his leg. "My friend? My friend? You have to be kidding. He was a total waste of air. You two did a service to society by taking him out."

Jones paused, looking into space as if considering how funny this was, a senseless grin crossing his face. As he relaxed, the barrel of the gun started to dip toward the ground. I had an opening. But with the first twitch of my leg, he broke out of his reverie and raised the gun to point at me. It was back to stalling.

"You can't hurt me with that gun," I said, hoping that the statement was discussion-worthy. I casually tried to slide closer to Diane, knowing that my claim applied to me, not her. But at the rate I could move without attracting Jones's attention, it would be an hour before she was inside the vest's protective field.

Jones laughed quietly, making my blood run cold. I preferred the bellowing, ranting version of the big man. "Jeremy, Jeremy, Jeremy. I know all about where I need to hit you. Shall we see just how long you can look me in the eye, while I pop off a few rounds at your head? One flinch, Jeremy ol' boy, and it's all over. Aren't you going to take a look if I wing your pretty, little doctor friend? We'll see how much good the vest does you then."

"Well, we ...." I started.

"Enough," Jones roared, the metamorphosis from quiet menace to full fury completed in the blink of an eye. "I don't give a damn what you have to say."

Perhaps we could ....

There was, however, a vulnerability, a potentially fatal flaw in the strategy that popped into my head. Diane had to read my mind because my plan would never work without her. I only hoped our time together had made that possible. I stole a sideways glance, not wanting to risk so much as a nod or a wink. In the background, I heard Jones continue his tirade. "I'll give you to three to get that vest off or Miss Pretty loses a knee. One ...."

Diane and I made eye contact and, in that instant, I saw a look that said 'I'm right behind you.' I wasn't sure my desperate gambit warranted her trust, but it was the only roll of the die I could picture.

I grabbed my chest, groaning and staggering away from Diane. To approach her would alert Jones; I just hoped she wouldn't misinterpret my act. But right on cue, she screamed, "Jeremy," and rushed toward me. It seemed an eternity, waiting for her to arrive, hoping the silence of the room would not be shattered by gunfire.

When she grabbed my arm to support me, the reprieve I felt was palpable. But that was just the first step. "He's ill," Diane shouted at Jones.

"What the hell difference does that make to me?" Jones yelled back, his eyes darting back and forth between the two of us with the gun following the same path. But his opportunity to shoot her was gone, as long as I faced him. So, I allowed Diane to pull me more upright.

"Lay me down, over there, above the couch," I croaked, barely nodding with my head to a spot about five feet away. The couch, of course, was one floor down, but the squeeze on my arm told me all I needed to know. She understood.

We hobbled the few feet to the spot I had indicated as Jones's patience was spent. "Just let him drop where he stands," Jones said, his lips curling into a snarl. "I ain't got all day."

I pulled Diane close and with a squeeze of my hand on her arm, we both flopped down, face-first onto the floor … only to past through to the level below.

Remembering to twist in mid-air, our fall ended on the first floor rather than in the basement. I missed the couch by about six inches, smashing an end table into a thousand pieces. Diane was more fortunate and landed mostly on it.

"Jeremy, are you all right?" she cried.

I sprung to my feet, more than willing to ignore the pain from the latest set of scrapes and bruises. I grabbed Diane's hand, saying, "I love you. Now, let's get out of here."

As if we needed any more encouragement, Jones's bellowing from above was followed by three cracks of the pistol, as chunks of the ceiling fell to the ground. He was obviously firing blindly, but he could still get lucky. We ran from the room. I grabbed her hand and pulled her close as we hit the back door. In the backyard, I said, "Without the tracking GPS, I know just how to lose him."

"Yeah, you told me," she said. "But let's stay outside the houses." Even in our frantic race from death, she wasn't going to let me forget.

I grinned at her and we took off. We zigged and zagged through backyards and parks. When hidden behind fences or hedgerows, I tried to keep the turns we made random. But overall, I kept angling away from Diane's house. After about a half hour, she pulled me to a stop.

"I don't think anyone could have followed that path. I'm certainly lost."

"Yeah, me too. But I'd guess we're at least a couple of miles from your place."

"Well, your apartment was off-limits before, and my house is now," said Diane. "So, I guess we need some temporary shelter to start. But after that? You have any ideas?"

"Not specifics, but there is one thing I'm sure about. We need to go on the offensive. We've just been reacting to their attacks, and frankly, I'm surprised our luck has held this long."

Diane's face showed concern, of course, but there was also a look of determination. "I agree," she said. "Together, we'll come up with something."

16. Connecting

The motel room was clean and functional, but little more. The queen-sized bed was covered in a floral print that could probably only be found in a catalog with the title of 'Vintage Bedding of the 1960s.' Hopefully, that meant a 60s style, not a 60s-manufacturing date. There was a chair, a dresser, and a television. We had rejected another place because it lacked a refrigerator and microwave, so we had those two items as well. If you added a few pictures on the wall, a hairdryer, a pad of paper and a pen, a couple of rolls of toilet paper, and a motel-size bar of soap and shampoo, you had a complete inventory of the room's contents.

Renting the room had taken the last of my cash and all that Diane had on her. Because we still felt that Benzinger and Jones didn't have connections beyond what a scientist and a common criminal would have, we were comfortable using our ATM and credit cards, although we didn't want to use them anywhere near our new home. After retrieving Diane's car—it was fortunate that she had parked it a block away—we drove halfway across town before we replenished our cash reserves. For now, at least, trying to get my car from her street was too much of a risk.

Diane called into her office, saying she had a family emergency and wouldn't be in for a few days. I hoped that was long enough. Then, we stopped by Walmart to get some clothes. It had exactly what we were seeking—volume at low cost.

"How about this six-pack of T-shirts on sale for $12?" I asked. "Just white, but I can go for a week with a pack of these and a pair of jeans."

"You going bare-chested on Sunday?" Diane leered at me, trying to cover her worry with humor, but I could tell.

"Get me a pack of mediums," she added.

"Men's?" I asked, tentatively.

"Sure. Why not? I'm certain we won't find a better price in the women's department."

And that's the way the clothes shopping went— underwear, socks, T-shirts, and a couple of pairs of jeans. We wanted to get enough clothes that we wouldn't have to go to the laundromat every other day if this went on for a while.

After that, it was the grocery store. Since we had extremely limited space in the refrigerator, it was a quick trip. This was one place we would need to visit every few days. In the interest of expanding my culinary horizons, we got some milk and a box of the chocolate, puffed cereal. After groceries, I topped off the gas tank, because you never knew when running out of gas before your pursuer might mean the end of your days. Maybe we were getting a bit savvier about life on the run, but we were probably just getting more paranoid.

Back at home, which had become wherever we planned to spend the night, we had dinner—a few veggies, bread, cheese, and some of the only wine I could find with a screw cap. It was, in a word, bad.

Afterward, we relaxed on the bed, resting side by side. Diane's breathing was deep and regular, but she was still awake; she was gently rubbing one of my arms. And as her fingertips lightly stroked my bare skin, my entire being receded to that point of contact. Gone were the trials of the last few days. Absent was the threat of tomorrow. In that moment, my life was the light caress of this amazing woman.

I turned my head toward her and her eyes opened, a sad smile coming to her lips. The warm tingle that had spread from her fingertips now seemed to radiate from my every sense—the deep pools of hazel from my eyes, the murmur of her breathing from my ears, the warmth of her body from my skin. I caressed her cheek with my hand. She drew close and we kissed lightly. I longed for the moment to last but knew it couldn't.

Diane dropped her eyes. "Jeremy?" She had spoken so softly that I almost didn't hear her.

"Yes?"

"I thought maybe we could try something ... different?"

I pulled back, wanting to see her face because I was thrown. She continued to look down. Was she really suggesting sex? Could she really compartmentalize her emotions so completely as to place our peril aside for a roll in the sack? I could, but then, I was male. A beautiful woman and privacy were more than enough to dominate my thoughts.

Then I realized, she was doing exactly the same as I—trying to live in the moment. We had been thrown together by my mistake and were on the cusp of placing our lives in each other's hands. Like me, she wanted to nourish our connection. It would help sustain us. It might be crucial for survival. And hopefully, it would be the start of memories we would recall fondly many years after this was over.

I was still wondering, however, if the 'different something' she wanted to try could actually be sex. So, I sat up and turned to face her, not knowing what to expect. An impish grin? A shy smile? But what I saw looked all the world to me like embarrassment. Her face was red and hands that just moments ago had been serenely massaging my arm now seemed in constant motion, as she clasped and unclasped them. I thought about saying, you can't possibly suggest anything I haven't dreamt of before, but that didn't sound like a good option. She might demand a list.

"You know," she finally said, "the vest lets objects merge in ways that don't happen, well, anywhere else on earth, as far as we know. What do you think it would be like for us to ... well, you know ... use it to merge ourselves?"

I was wrong. She had suggested something I had never dreamt of.

She continued. "When we realized that it was dangerous for me to be too far from you when we went through something solid, we talked about you keeping me close. I know you remember because you really hugged me tight when we were running from Jones this last time."

"Well, I was trying," I said. Actually, it had been foremost in my thoughts.

"And you did. It made me feel safer and I appreciate it. But a few of those times, I swear I was so close, I was ... part of you. I got this .... I don't know, like a rush of feelings that weren't my own or something. I know, we were running, I was scared, there were lots of things happening. But it seemed like more than just that."

"And you want to check it out in a quieter, less stressful setting?" I asked.

"Yes. I mean it might be possible that our thoughts, emotions, feelings, everything merges when we share the same space."

As she had spoken about the possibilities, her voice had become increasingly animated. She was curious about the promise of a deeper connection. The only problem was, the discussion was having the opposite effect on me. I was definitely having second thoughts. Diane was an amazing, striking woman. And as a result, there were all kinds of X-rated fantasies floating around in my head involving her and not just in my unconscious. Maybe she hadn't considered the consequences of this mind-meld.

"Assuming it works, are you certain you're ready to experience what I'm experiencing? Think what I'm thinking?" I asked, watching her face closely. There was no hesitation in her response.

"It may not even work that way," she said. "Just because you're wearing the vest, I'm not sure it means that your thoughts and feelings become mine. It might be that we end up with a shared experience."

I swallowed hard, as my stomach rolled. She'd thought it through to the point that she was even willing to share her thoughts with me. I couldn't get the image of Diane slapping me in the face and storming out the door the instant our 'merge' started.

My worries must have shown on my face. "Jeremy Reynolds, are you afraid to let me see inside your head?" I guess my hesitation was all the answer that she needed.

"I'm not going to recount every time a guy tried to jump me at the end of a first date ... or even in the middle of one, just to make you comfortable. But let me assure you, nothing in your thoughts will shock me."

I made a mental note to ask about what had happened once in the middle of a first date, but that was a discussion for another time. Right now, I had other concerns. "You can't be sure about that," I said.

"No more than you can be sure it won't work the other way and you'll be shocked by me."

I laughed. "Not likely."

She shrugged and thought for a moment. "Look, I put the kibosh on blowing stuff up with the vest," she said mildly, evenly. "If you're uncomfortable with this, we don't have to do it."

She didn't look happy with the offer, but on the other hand, she hadn't gamed the situation either. She hadn't even said something like, 'if you are uncomfortable getting to know me better,' which would have made her offer impossible for me to refuse. She had been direct and upfront, qualities I admired. She had also offered me the chance to connect more closely with someone who I liked and whose wants and needs I would know and could respond to instantly. And she could do the same for me. The thought was immensely exciting and enormously scary at the same time.

"Do you want to change places and wear the vest?" I asked. "If thoughts only go one way, you won't have to be psychologically scarred by my debauchery."

She smiled and punched me lightly in the arm. After a moment's thought, she said, "No, you can see my fantasies first, if that's the way it works."

Internally, I groaned. Mentioning her fantasies was not the thing to say if she was really going to see my thoughts in a few seconds.

We stood up from the bed and faced each other. "OK, I'll start with a quick step in and out at first. Get you used to my depravity slowly."

I turned the vest on. We were only inches apart. This perspective alone was more than enough to have my mind churning, but not from anything the vest was doing. I slowly leaned forward for just a second and withdrew.

"Anything?" I asked.

"No. You?"

"Nothing. Shall we try again, a little more forward and a little longer?" I asked.

"OK, but hold on a sec." She took the spread off the bed, folded it several times, and placed it on the floor. She stepped on top. Now, we were eye-to-eye and would be brain-to-brain when merged. I blinked a couple of times, wondering if this was the step that would make it all happen.

I stepped forward into Diane again, holding the spot for a second or two. But when I stepped back, we each reported the same results. Nothing.

"OK," Diane said, "this time, start behind me. Move forward until we are fully aligned. Then hold that spot for, say, ten seconds. If we still feel nothing, I think we have our answer."

"From behind?" I put both hands over my mouth in an exaggerated look of shock. "Maybe I will be stunned when I see inside your mind."

"Jeremy, I swear I don't know what I'm going to do with you." She grinned.

"I'll tell you your thoughts on that topic in just a few seconds."

She was still on the mound of bedspread. I positioned myself behind her so that when I stepped forward, our heads would be at the same height and orientation. I swallowed hard, my hands starting to sweat from the prospect of what might soon happen. I moved forward.

As I stood there counting to ten in the gray blur, I tried to search the void with my mind. Was Diane in here, somewhere? I sensed nothing. I wondered what she might be experiencing. And if it was anything, would she be willing to take the vest and trade roles. But as I stepped forward and turned, she was already shaking her head, her lips pressed together tightly in a line.

"Nothing," she said, her shoulders slumping. "It was as if you weren't there. And since you're not asking for a cigarette, I'm guessing it was the same for you."

"Yeah, I'm sorry, sugar, but nothing."

"Well, it was worth a try," she said. And she sighed. I felt bad because she did, but part of me was relieved.

"From a scientific point of view, it was a disappointing result," I said. "But from a personal perspective, our old-fashioned approach has been pretty mind-blowing."

She smiled, cupping my cheek in her hand. We laid back down on the bed. She laid her head on my shoulder, while I wrapped her in my arms. With the weightiness of our failed experiment, it was difficult to think of anything to say. Flattery, however, had always worked, especially when true.

"Did I mention how impressive your mind-reading act was, when we escaped from Jones," I said after a while.

She gave a single, soft laugh, snuggling closer. "About twenty times, but thanks. But it's you who saved our skin with that fall-through-the-floor trick. What's that, a couple of dozen times you've saved us?"

"I think you need to brush up on your math. You're going to need a good accountant to do your books if that's the way you add."

"I know for a fact that Dr. Weathers' brother does his books now, and he's as old as Ralph. Older, in fact. The job's all yours if you want it."

"Wow." I drew back far enough to see her face, checking that she wasn't joking. "Yeah, sure, I'll take it. That was the easiest job interview I've ever had."

"Well, I may not be totally objective when it comes to you." She pulled me back closer, burying her head again in my shoulder. That brought a smile to my face. "But there's something I don't understand. You told me you are an accountant, but you've mostly been doing temporary jobs, and none of those are in accounting."

"I did say that," I replied.

"But just now, you said you'd do the accounting for the clinic, and you sounded interested."

"I am. I wasn't really fishing for a job, but my offer to do the books was completely serious. I'd have to look at them to be certain, but assuming that Dr. Weathers isn't doing something like running an illegal pot business through the clinic, I'd love to work for you. So, are you wondering about my change of heart?"

"Yeah, that's part of it," she said.

"It just feels like it's time for me to get back to something more than the temp jobs." I hugged her a little tighter, feeling very safe telling her some of my dreams.

"Is that where you're going, back to a career in accounting? I just ask, because .... Well, you seem to have a background that's littered with science. Those anomalous thrust devices. Or electrophoresis. Not many people have even heard of either of those."

"I wasn't always interested in accounting. When I started college, I was in a pre-veterinary medicine program."

"Really?" This time, it was Diane who drew back to look into my eyes. "Why the change?" she asked, as she propped herself up on an elbow, watching me.

"After my freshman year, my parents died. Car crash, drunk driver. But it wasn't like they left me penniless or anything. In fact, after all the legal dust settled, I had enough money to cover four years of undergraduate school. But when I looked at the cost of vet school, which would be another four years at nearly twice the price, I couldn't see a way to make it work. Even with part-time jobs during school, full-time in the summers, and keeping the scholarships I had, I'd be so loaded with debt, I figured I'd never get out."

"Didn't you have any relatives that could help?" asked Diane, as she continued to watch my face. "I'll be working off my loans for medical school for several more years, but I would have been a lot deeper in debt if my folks hadn't helped me."

"I have a boatload of cousins. In fact, now that I think about it, I don't know how I ended up as an only child the way my mom's and dad's brothers and sisters multiplied like rabbits."

"Ugh, that's a terrible thing to say about your kin," Diane said, as she allowed her head to flop down on my shoulder. I immediately wrapped her in a hug, wanting to keep her close.

"They know it. Anyway, they had their own problems getting their kids through school. So, through the eyes of a 19-year-old, who was more than a bit concerned about his own uncertain future, the direct path of business school seemed the best bet."

"So, you knew about electrophoresis because of some freshman chemistry class you took before you switched to business?" asked Diane.

"I did, although the definition is all I remember about it."

Diane was quiet a moment, apparently considering what she had heard. "So, maybe I'm reading this wrong, but it sounds like you went into accounting so you could save for vet school."

Do I really want to tell her the whole story?

I knew the answer was yes almost before the question had fully formed in my mind. "I don't think I've ever said this to anyone else, but yeah, that was the dream. But then, I got out into the real world and things changed. I had a serious girlfriend; we lived together for almost four years. My accounting work became the way we made a place for ourselves. Our future, as I saw it, gave the work some meaning. But she and I didn't last. We wanted different things out of life. After we split up, work became pointless and frankly, I started drifting."

"And you didn't consider going back to your original plan, use your accounting background to fund vet school?" asked Diane.

"That's a good question, and if I hadn't been thinking about it recently, I probably couldn't have answered. But it wasn't that I decided not to go back to my plan. I just didn't decide anything. My old dreams seemed to be gone."

Without raising her head from my shoulder, she looked up at me. "You know, it's not too late." Then, she paused for a second, her forehead wrinkling, and said, "But then, you've been thinking about going back to work to fund school already, haven't you?"

"OK, I'm getting a little freaked out now," I said. "To this point, I could see why you thought what you did. There were things in what I had said, clues if you will. But how did you know I was thinking about that?"

She dropped her eyes and snuggled in closer. "I wasn't certain, of course, but you were interested in doing the books for my practice. But it wasn't that so much as the interest you show whenever we discuss anything medical. Or scientific. You don't shy away from those discussions. In fact, you often start them. And then, re-thinking your life probably makes a lot of sense in our current situation. Not to be too melodramatic, but looking into the face of death would make anyone think about what they want in the time they have left."

"No kidding," I said, knowing that she was close to the truth, but not quite there. Sure, I was thinking about things differently with the threat we were facing. But my renewed drive to succeed was the result of seeing what she was doing with her life, not my own mortality. She made me want to do better.

I pulled her closer, and a tiny murmur of contentment escaped her lips. "Yeah, it's been nip and tuck the last few days, but we have at least 80 more years. And yes, I'm thinking about what I want in them."

And what I want is you.

I left that part of my dream unspoken.

17. The best-laid plans

After a few more minutes in each other's arms, Diane said, "It'd be nice to lay here all night. But maybe we should be thinking about a way out of our predicament?" She stood and looked down at me.

"Such a hard task-master," I teased, as I started to climb out of bed. But just as I was getting up, she pushed me and I fell back. She stood over me, grinning.

I rolled off the other side, ran around the end, chased her into a corner, and wrapped her in a bear hug. I picked her up and started carrying her toward the bed, gasping not from the exertion—Diane was light—but because breathing was coming second to laughter.

Diane giggled, saying, "Jeremy, put me down. You'll wake the neighbors."

I sat her down on the floor, but kept my arms around her waist, looking down into her eyes. Her cheeks were flushed from our wrestling. "It's 7:00 o'clock. No one's sleeping. Besides, I can ravish you quietly."

"You're bad," she said with that impish grin of hers. She kissed me lightly, then wiggled out of my arms. "But seriously, we should probably get started."

I thought about protesting, saying that I had tried before her sneak attack, but she was right. Playtime was over, at least for a while.

I had never planned how to overcome a brilliant but deranged scientist and his dutiful minion, but I had worked on any number of other complex issues—moves, career decisions, what brand of light bulbs to buy. I was a 'lists' man, relying heavily on the pros and cons of an issue to organize my thoughts. I had mentioned that fact to Diane at Walmart while purchasing a few aids—several large sheets of paper, a couple of markers, and a roll of masking tape.

When I pulled them out and taped a couple of sheets of paper on a wall, Diane said, "Ah, the infamous lists. You know, I'm more of a seat of your pants decision-maker. Well, not professionally," she added quickly as if I might think less of her if she didn't do doctoring by the book.

"And that's perfect," I said. "I saw you pick Benzinger's lab out of the warren of rooms at Frontier. So, I'm betting that one of these lists ends with 'Diane's gut says do this'. And that's exactly what we want. Opposite decision styles leading to the perfect answer. And, we have the added benefit that ...."

"Opposites attract," she said, finishing the thought for me. And so, the process began. Part of the time, the discussion was weighty.

"We could buy a couple of handguns, get safety training, practice at the range," I said at one point.

Diane had picked up the motel pen and she was absentmindedly tapping it on the side of her head, as she paced back and forth. I had the feeling that she was playing out scenes in her mind by the way she often responded to these options.

"I don't think I can," she said finally, frowning at me. "I'm sure I have steady hands and could probably be a good shot ...." She paused, wincing, perhaps at the image in her head. "But I think I'd hesitate, maybe not even be able to pull the trigger at all. And besides, as long as he is facing us with the vest, a gun is useless anyway." She looked down and started pacing again.

And part of the time, the discussion involved pure flights of fancy.

"How about we slip them some LSD?" I asked, trying to keep a straight face.

Diane stifled a laugh with her hand. "What, we're going to keep them dosed up for the rest of our lives?"

"Sure, get them signed up for one of those meal-delivery services and you doctor up the package each week. Sixty years of that should cover us." I was still trying to look serious, but it was becoming difficult the way she was rolling her eyes. Then, she buried her head in my chest, and I could feel her shoulders shake as she continued to titter.

But overall, the discussion was serious and it took a toll. Diane alternated between pacing, tapping that pen on anything in reach, and sitting down on the edge of the bed while she ran a hand through her hair. The frivolous ideas gave us a break, but overall, we were focusing on our vulnerabilities and that's a tough thing to think about for long.

After a couple of hours, it was clear that we kept circling back to the same ideas.

"So, it looks like the best options boil down to exploiting Jones as the weaker link," I said, "and getting him to admit to some type of connection to Schmidt."

This seemed the only way to keep Benzinger from profiting from the vest. Without a connection to something criminal, he would eventually develop the technology, become rich, and take his revenge when we didn't expect it. His bizarre tale at the Science Center had convinced me of that.

Diane was sitting on the edge of the bed, shoulders slumped, wringing her hands. She was incredibly strong, but everyone had their limit. And she was approaching hers. We needed to make a decision, even if it was to put this off for now. That option, however, was not preferable in my mind. I was worried that the stress would accumulate and we'd end up paralyzed by fear.

I sat down on the bed next to her and wrapped an arm around her shoulders. "We don't need much from Jones. Just his real name might be enough. With a name, the police can find him and I'll bet he'll turn on Benzinger before it's over."

"But can't we just get a private investigator to find out who he is?" She stared down at her hands, as they had finally come to rest in her lap. I was about to answer when she said, "I know, we've talked about that. With as little as we could give a PI, it'll take forever to find Jones. We end up living out of a motel or making my place a fortress with bodyguards to follow me to work every day." She continued to look down.

I took my other arm and encircled her shoulders, leaning my head against hers. "We'll work it out, sugar. We've outmaneuvered Jones four times already, all with no planning. We'll be prepared this time."

Diane said nothing, but I felt her shoulders rise and fall in a deep sigh. I was about to suggest we break for the day, when she said, "OK, just the details, one more time?"

I ended the hug and took her hands in mine, hoping she would look up at me. She did, and smiled, her lips tight in the effort.

"One, we let Benzinger see us at the Great River Trail South where, according to him, he jogs at lunchtime," I said. "That lets us know when and where Jones will be, assuming that Benzinger calls immediately after spotting us. And he should because he won't want us to get away."

Diane just nodded, still looking at me. She had slipped her hands from mine and she was rubbing them on her knees.

"Second, we get any kind of admission from him—his name, his connection to Benzinger, something about the crime, anything. This seems like the easiest part of the plan to me. He loves to brag. I just need to be wired so that we get it on tape."

"I don't know why you have to do that. I could get him to talk as easily as you. And you could hide off to one side, where he's vulnerable."

We had discussed this too, and I was certain she hadn't forgotten. I think she was just hoping for a different answer to the same question. "Me wearing the wire is our best shot, and I'm not just saying that because of some macho thing. If you're the one that's wired, Jones will be bragging alright, but it'll be about his sexual prowess. No one wants a tape of that."

In my mind, however, this aspect of our plan was critical, not just some nice-to-have, better-case alternative. She was fond of telling me about how I had saved her life. But in fact, she wouldn't need saving if it wasn't for me. She wasn't going to face Jones again if I had anything to say about it. Period. End of story.

"Then, we have the primary plan and the backup," I said, picking up where we had left off. "The primary is to use a preplanned escape route to any one of our four safe spots." These locations were just public areas near the trail where Jones would not be able to attack me, including one police substation. I wanted to avoid a repeat of the fruitless search I had experienced before. We had even planned routes to these spots that would minimize my exposure.

We had also come up with three possible defenses against the vest. They came into the plan at this point. "To give myself a head start, I'll try the water, the pepper spray, or the sonic defender on him. Or some combination of them."

Neither hitting him with the pepper spray nor dousing him with water, which we hoped would make him hesitate to use the vest's electronics, were strong options in my opinion. That was because attacking him with anything from a peashooter to a hand grenade was problematic; the vest would render them ineffective as long as he faced the onslaught. That left an attack to a very small part of his body, his ears. I guessed it was their shape that kept them from being shielded by the device, but all I knew for sure was that I could hear fine when wearing the vest.

Diane was perched on the edge of the bed and was sitting still for now. "The sonic defender will be your best bet because it'll work from any angle," she said, putting my thoughts into words. I was about to agree when she added, "And it's probably better if you hold it at arm's length. Anything to get it a little farther from your ears." Again, I was about to say we were on the same page when she added, "And if your other hand is free, you might want to cover one ear with it and turn your head so the other ear isn't exposed."

She had treated someone hit by a Sonic Defender and had developed a healthy respect for its capabilities. After all her warnings, I had too.

Diane got up from the bed, found the pen she had left on the dresser, and started twirling it between her fingers as she paced back and forth across the room. "It's the backup plan that worries me. This whole thing about trapping Jones in an abandoned, industrial building. Are you sure you want to build a fault into our vest? I mean, it's been our lifeline."

I thought about getting off the bed, tracking her down, and wrapping her in my arms. But it seemed like she needed to walk off the nervous energy. So, I stayed seated.

"I'm just putting a fuse that is somewhat too small into the circuit. It runs for a few seconds, meaning we can use the vest, but we can't leave it on. But if I get Jones into our vest, he goes into one of the old buildings and searches for a few moments, he'll be trapped. The trick, of course, is getting him into our vest, which is why I hope to douse him with the water. It won't short out his vest, but he'll be worried about it and want to use ours."

"I don't know anything about electronics," Diane protested, frowning from across the room.

"And I don't know much either, but we test all of this out in advance. If it doesn't work, we come up with a new idea."

Diane stopped pacing and looked at me. "And there's several of these old buildings out along the trail?"

I nodded. "Yeah, we're right by the river. There are all kinds of old manufacturing and storage buildings out there."

"But he won't leave you outside alone. He'll take you in with him," said Diane, frowning.

"Probably. But despite the snarling and posturing, Jones is a businessman. If he's trapped, he's not going to follow through without any hope of pay." I suspected he might punch me a few times out of frustration, but I really doubted that he would seriously hurt me while we waited for the police to arrive.

Diane sat down hard in our one chair, her hand starting to massage her forehead. I hated to continue, but we were to the last step. "Finally, whatever we get on tape—Jones's name, Jones himself trapped in the building, a reference to his association with Benzinger, whatever. You take it to Underwood. You play the recording for him and he brings in the cavalry."

And this, in my mind was the second crucial piece of our plan. She couldn't endanger herself, doing the equivalent of a dash across I-64 because she thought I was in trouble. She had to stay safe, far from Jones, in order to bring our evidence to the police. I hoped it was fool-proof, but I worried it wasn't.

Diane was still sitting, still trying to massage the tension out of her forehead. I got up off the bed, walked over, and knelt in front of her so I could look into her eyes. "We can knock off for the night and brainstorm options again tomorrow if you want. Maybe there's something we've overlooked. Or when we wake up, we can go shopping for what we need for this plan and make sure it works flawlessly. We're not going out there until we're ready."

She stopped rubbing her head and looked at me. "Shopping, I guess. Isn't that what the woman always opts to do?" She gave me a sardonic smile.

"So, are you getting tired?" I asked, still kneeling in front of her. I raised my eyebrows, putting enough of a hopeful look on my face to be certain she understood what I was really asking.

She took a hand and ran it down my cheek. "You're sweet, honey, but I'd be a terrible partner tonight. And I don't want that. I'm just too distracted by all that could go wrong and what that might mean. Tonight, would it be OK if I just slept in your arms? And then, tomorrow night, we'll make up for it."

"Absolutely," I said.

In truth, I was relieved. I couldn't have done justice to the passion I felt for her either. The need to show calm confidence during our talk had left my stomach churning, my muscles in a knot. Perhaps after a shower I could get some sleep, confident in the belief that I would be able to shelter Diane from Jones.

But then, that's what I had thought at the mall.

18. Nineteen seconds

We had been awake since 4:00 AM. To get everything completed, we needed my car. So, after watching her house for nearly an hour, and seeing no movement, save those in other homes where people were getting ready for work, I slipped into my car and drove off. No problems so far.

We split up our shopping list. I took the part with the commercial electronics, and so, could take advantage of the holiday store hours that many of the chains were already using. Shopping completed, I was back at the motel by 8:00 AM, working on the 'wire,' as we were calling it.

In fact, the wire was nothing more than a wireless headset. We had researched online until we found one that was known for having an extremely sensitive microphone. I now paired it to my phone and put Diane's number on speed dial. The idea was that as soon as Jones arrived, I'd hit speed dial, and we would capture everything he said on her voicemail. Not particularly high-tech espionage, but cheap and reliable.

Then, I called her cell service carrier and found out how to make a call go directly to voicemail so we wouldn't miss a single word of his pearls of wisdom. I also wanted Diane to be able to listen while the call was being recorded, so she would know exactly when Jones had incriminated himself. I was afraid that might not be possible, or at least difficult, but her carrier knew exactly how to do it as if they got that question every day.

Just as I hung up, she came through the door.

"How'd the shopping go?" I asked. I was already thinking that the answer would be 'not good,' because she was scowling.

"I got the fuses, the soldering iron, and the solder, but don't ask me to go back there again."

"Why not?"

She had shucked off her jacket and stood there in one of the white T-shirts, rubbing one arm. "There are these two guys who work there, and they act like they've never had a woman come in their store before."

"It's possible you're the first," I said, only half in jest. "The place is a throwback to the days of vacuum tubes, but they carry stuff no one else has. It's probably not big as a destination for girls' night out." Then, I looked at her T-shirt.

Diane had evidently caught the drift of my gaze and looked down. "You have to be kidding. I'm wearing a bra."

"I'd told you that you'd be surprised by what's in a guy's mind." Her eyes narrowed, but before she could give me any trouble, I moved on. "I just need to do a little programming on your voicemail, and we'll be ready to check out the wire."

"OK, I'll start working on the fuses," she said.

If we had known more about electricity, we probably could have determined exactly what size of fuse we needed. But we didn't. So instead, Diane opened the vest and we found the specifications for the battery stamped on its side.

At that point, we had the amperage and knew approximately what was required. Then, we bought an assortment of fuses that would be likely to burn out during normal operation. We just needed one that would last 10 or 15 seconds before that happened.

"Done with the programming," I said to Diane, flashing her a grin. That had gone better than I ever expected. "Whenever you want to test it, we can."

"No time like the present." She sounded much more upbeat than just a moment ago. "Do you have the tape to put it on your chest?"

"I thought we could just lay it on the dresser and stand across the room to see how sensitive it is."

"No, let's do this right." Now her tone was definitely light, and I saw a smile on her lips. "Ah, here's the tape. Now strip off that shirt."

She knew my body well, of course, but to this point, it had been from fumbling in the dark. The command to undress in front of her had my heart pounding and my face warming almost instantly. I thought about saying, 'after you,' but more ribbing was all I was likely to get in response. So, I removed my shirt, making a production of it.

She whistled, grinning at me. "Any place you're less attached to your chest hair?"

"I was never too wild about this spot," I said, touching an area just below the neckline of my shirt.

She continued to grin at me, attaching the headset and stepping across the room. I hit speed dial on my phone.

Diane started speaking. "Testing ... oh, there's a slight lag. I can't talk into the phone and listen at the same time."

"That's probably good enough," I said.

She dialed voicemail and replayed her message on her phone's speaker. "Testing ... oh, there's a slight lag. I can't talk into the phone and listen at the same time."

"Not bad," I said, nodding at her. "But the microphone is so sensitive, I can hear myself breathing. And I think that was me swallowing."

"Putting it a little lower and off-center should help with that," Diane said. She delivered that statement with all the clinical precision of a medical doctor. And then, she rubbed her hands together, grinned suggestively, and said, "Shall I remove the tape? I'll be gentle. Not."

"Is this the bedside manner they teach you in med school?"

"No, it's my own special brand, just for you." She continued to leer at me.

"Sure, you can take it off, but that's enough testing in place," I said.

Of course, she spoiled the entire illusion that she was enjoying this bit of slap to go with, hopefully, a tickle later when she squeezed her eyes shut before pulling off the tape. I laughed. She shrugged, saying, "Yeah, I'm not really into hurting people."

Diane went back to testing the fuses. After a while, she said, "I think I've identified the best one of the bunch. None of them burn out at 10 seconds like you hoped." She held up a fuse and said, "These last about 23 seconds, with the fastest burning out in about 19 seconds and the slowest at about 28. If I use a fuse at the next higher value, they don't burn out until after a minute."

"We can live with 19 seconds, but I wish there wasn't so much difference between the shortest and longest times. How many are left?"

"Just one. I used up most of them in testing. Would you mind going back to that store? If I go back, I'll tell those two guys off."

"Sure, no problem. And when I get back, we can decide if we go today or not. I believe everything's ready, but if you want to think about it for a while, we can do that."

△ △ △

"We're going to have to pay for that."

"What?" Diane asked, looking at me blankly.

"The hole you're making in the carpet from pacing back and forth."

"I'm sorry," she said, "but this is nerve-racking."

She sat down beside me on the edge of the bed. For a moment, I missed the couch back in her house where she would sit on her feet and snuggle up against me. But then, she was too agitated and I was too tense for either of us to sit long anyway.

I had picked up the extra fuses, and then we had walked through the plan and the risks again. Everything was in place. "Do you want to test another fuse?" I asked.

She got up from the bed and paced to the far wall and back. Ten steps total, round trip. It's all the room she had. She looked down at me. "No. The fuses are fine. And the recording set up is fine, too. Everything's fine. It's the stuff we can't predict that worries me."

I reached out and took her hands. She nodded her head, just once, forcefully. "OK. Let's do this."

"Are you sure?" I asked.

She nodded again, a tight smile on her face. "No, but let's go before I change my mind. We can find our site, and if everything still looks good, we'll let Benzinger spot us when he goes for his run."

In many ways, it was amazing that I hadn't been there on the carpet right beside her, pacing back and forth. A crack had appeared in my plan this morning, and I was none too happy about it. It involved how Diane might react while listening in on our conversation. I had tried to convince her to go to the police station. She and Detective Underwood could listen to the conversation live, there in the safe confines of his office.

But she would have none of it. She agreed to stay hidden, but wanted to be nearby, 'just in case.' And therein was my concern. Just what were these cases that required her presence? Asking her got me nowhere.

So, after racking my brain and coming up with no plans less likely to produce these emergencies, I decided to trust her judgment. And I did because I knew no one more level-headed than Diane.

We gathered our jackets, as the weather was clear but cool, and headed for the car. It was only a short drive, and soon we were hiking along the trail, looking for possible buildings to use as a trap. Diane seemed to have turned the corner from nervous fretting to single-minded determination, as she clinically dissected the pros and cons of each structure we passed. If she had intentionally decided to throw herself into the task as a distraction, it was working beautifully. She seemed much calmer than I felt.

After discarding a few options, we found a building that had probably been some type of storage for grain, like a small, rectangular silo. It was constructed of poured concrete, measuring about 6 by 50 feet at the base and rising about 35 feet into the air. What made it perfect was the fact it had only two openings at ground level. Both were heavy steel doors that were chained and padlocked. They would not be easy to defeat without a vest.

Other than these doors, there were four other openings of about five by five feet, located about 25 feet above ground level. There were two on the front of the building, above the two steel doors, and two directly across from them on the back.

"I'll go in through here first," I said, pointing to the door on the right. "I should be back in a moment." Diane nodded.

I powered up the vest and stepped in. But passing wasn't as simple as I expected. The structure was filled with something, so all I could see was confusing grayness. Trying to turn around and come back out the door was an option, but it was easy to get disoriented. So, I went straight ahead, emerging on the other side of the building after several seconds. Then, I walked around the end of the structure to find Diane still standing by the door.

"What happened to you?" she asked, running up to meet me. "You've been gone for almost a minute."

"Yeah, sorry. This side's not empty, so I went on through. We must be right at the six-foot limit of the vest because it took me a while. I'll try the other door and if that side's full too, we'll have to find another place."

As soon as I stepped through the second door, I knew we had found our trap. "Diane?" I yelled through the door.

"Yeah."

"It's perfect. I'll come get you."

Once she was inside with me, she said, "Look, a ladder."

"Oh, yeah. I didn't see that, but it makes sense. Whoever owns this place probably doesn't want anyone getting stuck in here accidentally. We'll need to remove it, of course."

Over the next several minutes, we explored and prepared the building. Internally, the 50-foot width of the silo was divided equally into two parts, forming two 6 by 25-foot spaces each with their own steel door. The area I had entered first was filled with construction waste—pieces of beams, rebar, crumbled concrete, and the like.

On our side of the building about a foot below the five by five-foot windows, a beam ran across the room, front to back. It was still over 20 feet above the ground, so before we removed the ladder, I coiled a rope on top of it. From the ground, the rope wasn't visible. To retrieve it from below, I tied a piece of fishing line on one end and ran it to the floor in one corner of the room. If you didn't know the line was there, you'd never spot it against the rough texture of the walls. It was ingenious enough that I almost hoped that Jones would try to imprison me there, while he searched for Diane. I'd be out of the building in a flash.

After that, we hauled the ladder out one of the windows. It wasn't really heavy, but it was unwieldy in the confined space, and we were breathing hard by the time we got it out. We carried it about 40 yards from the silo and hid it in some weeds.

We were all set.

We sat down on a large chunk of concrete, about 25 feet from our building. I put my arm around Diane. Her cheeks were pink from the effort of the last hour or so. Her hair was straying in front of her eyes from the light breeze.

"Thanks," she said. "I was warm, wrestling with that ladder, but I'm getting cold already just sitting here."

"Yeah, me too," I said. "It's a little early, but want a snack? It'll warm you up."

"Sure."

I broke out some cheese, bread, and fruit we had brought, spreading it out on our concrete table. "Too bad I forgot our wine," I said, wanting to see Diane's reaction. She made a face like she had just taken a sip of vinegar.

After we had eaten, we found a spot on a log to take up our surveillance. The wood felt warmer than the concrete, and I sat with Diane on my lap, my arms wrapped around her. She snuggled up to me, saying, "Mmm, you're warm."

True to form, at one point this morning, I had slipped and dropped to one knee. Unfortunately, it was in the middle of a mud puddle. The pants I saw beyond where Diane sat were caked with grime. Then, as she drew her hand up near her face, a gap appeared between her jacket and glove. I saw she had scraped her wrist.

"How'd you hurt yourself?" I asked.

"It's nothing. Just slipped once coming down the ladder. Here, you can kiss it and make it all better." And she held it up for me, smiling.

"You know, we're a little banged up, dirty, and cold. Want to go back to the motel, get some rest, and spring this trap tomorrow?" I asked.

She tilted her head, looking up at me and said, "If you can hold me like this to keep me warm, I'm fine. I don't need another sleepless night if we can get this over with today."

"OK," I said. I checked my watch. "I don't know what lunchtime means to Benzinger, but it's almost noon now."

The way we were positioned, Diane was looking up the trail in one direction and I was looking down it in the other. Neither of us said anything for quite some time. Occasionally, Diane would squeeze a little closer or play a hand across my leg. And in turn, I would occasionally rub my hand up and down her arm, like I was trying to warm her up. Maybe it did, but I just wanted the contact. Otherwise, we were quiet and still.

After a while, Diane reached in the pocket of her jacket and pulled out a headband. "My ears are a little cold," she said, as she pulled it on. She moved closer and we went quiet again.

When 1:30 arrived, I was ready to call a halt, believing that Benzinger had found something else to do today. But just as I was about ready to suggest that we regroup tomorrow, Diane whispered, "Here he comes."

We both stood and I turned around. Sure enough, there was Benzinger, trudging down the path. We started milling around outside our grain-silo-turned-trap, intending to catch Benzinger's attention as he passed us. Before long, he was close enough that we could hear his footsteps. Then, he reached a point directly across from us. The building was only about 20 yards from the trail, but Benzinger seemed oblivious to his surroundings. As he started to move away, Diane shouted, "Hey, Jeremy. Look at that window up there." She was pointing at the opening.

Hopefully, her action didn't seem contrived, because Benzinger had finally stopped to look. Then, from the corner of my eye, I could see him move off the path and pull out his phone. There was no doubt he had recognized us.

"What's on the other side?" I asked, and grabbed Diane's hand as we stepped out of his view. "That was great. Definitely got his attention."

Diane was frowning at me, clasping her hands in front of her. "Well, for better or worse, Jones will be here soon."

"For the better. Trust me, it's for the better."

I was running on adrenaline, talking a little too fast, shifting from foot to foot about every half second, like the rocks under my feet had suddenly become a little too hot for me to stand still. I told myself to slow down, clear the head, and think. Rushing into this confrontation would just get us hurt.

I peered around the corner of the structure and saw Benzinger scurrying back the way he had come. Turning to Diane, I stepped forward and we embraced, holding onto each other for several minutes, neither of us saying a word. I could hear my heartbeat. It was back to normal. I could feel Diane's. It was rock solid. She was an amazing woman.

"You need to come back to me," was all she said.

"I will," I replied. But in my mind, I wondered if these were the last words I would ever say to her.

19. A meeting of the minds

It didn't take long for Jones to show up. Nor was it hard to spot him when he did. He was coming down the middle of the trail in plain sight. I didn't like the looks of this at all. I took a deep breath, releasing it slowly, reminding myself that I didn't need much—just a name or even a location at the wrong time. I hit speed dial for Diane's voicemail, just as he arrived.

He pulled a gun from his pocket; I had expected that. He was again dressed in black, with a sweatshirt replacing the ever-present T-shirt. But the muscles were still evident, as were the lumps from his vest underneath. "Hey, Jeremy ol' boy. Where's the good-looking doc? I've missed her."

"She's inside," I said, nodding at the structure. Just as well prepare him for the backup plan if things go that far. Jones was dangerous, but I still felt good about our chances against him. I focused on what needed to be done.

"And you're out here with the vest? What's she doing, settin' a trap for me?" asked Jones, grinning.

"Naw, you know how it is with these women, all those domestic instincts. I think she's doing some housekeeping."

I had to keep telling myself to keep my hand away from the vest's power switch. I felt naked, facing him without it being on. But I had to use the vest sparingly or the fuse would burn out before Jones ever put it on. I took a deep breath, releasing it quietly so Jones wouldn't notice.

"Even I don't believe anything that stupid," Jones said, his lip curling into a snarl.

"Sure, you do," I said. Jones glared at me. I wasn't certain, but anger seemed to loosen his tongue. "So, am I going to my grave, not even knowing whose name I should be cursing for an eternity?"

"Don't say anything, Tom," said a new voice from the side of the silo. "He can curse my name for an eternity if that's what he wants."

"Benzinger," I said, as his name escaped my lips involuntarily. I squeezed my eyes closed for a moment as if I could push him from this nightmare. He had appeared at the corner of the silo, gun in hand. He must have snuck through the trees, brush, and tall grass that ran parallel to the trail. The mud on his shoes and a couple of twigs in his tweed jacket seemed to confirm that guess. He was dressed the part of the conservative academic, even if he was here to kill me.

"Indeed. You even have the correct name this time," he intoned in his thick accent.

For the fifth time in five encounters, Benzinger and Jones were one step ahead of me and my heart started beating out of my chest. The only good thing was that Benzinger hadn't bumped into Diane. She was still safely hidden away, and by design, even I didn't know her exact location. But if he came along the tree line behind the silo, he must have been very close to her hiding spot.

I knew my penchant for analysis was really no match for the eons of genetic programming that put fight or flight at the top of my mind. I had been able to redirect some of that energy in the previous encounters, but I had worked on an even better form of compensation for this meeting. Routine. Since the moment we had devised our plan, I had run over it, piece by piece, step by step in my mind. It was burned into my brain. It was the checklist that a pilot executes flawlessly in the middle of a nosedive to save a plane full of passengers because his actions had become second nature.

And so, I raced through my emergency checklist. Pepper spray—forget it. It would never work on two of them. Water, out. Benzinger would just laugh, knowing everything was waterproof. Vest, out unless I could get both of them on the same side of me. And then, I'd only be safe for nineteen seconds. Wire, doubtful, but it was worth a try. That left the sonic defender as my only defense in full play.

My limited arsenal seemed to nudge my heart rate a notch higher. I wiped my sweaty palms on my jeans and did my best to focus on actions not named fight or flight. Since Benzinger wouldn't have much patience for stalling, I needed to get something on tape fast.

"So, just what is it you're going to be doing with the vest anyway? Dr. Stapleton has some wild ideas about new materials or something. Me, I still think it'll just replace those automatic doors you see at grocery stores." I thought calling his baby ugly might work.

"I'm not certain what you mean, Mr. Reynolds. I usually don't wear vests at all, preferring a two-piece suit. Vests seem so old-fashioned."

That pretty much answered my question. He wasn't going to be goaded into an admission, which left the sonic defender as my best and only line of defense. Unfortunately, the defender was on my right side, which was the same side as Benzinger. With little else to try, I slowly raised my hand toward the pocket.

"I'd stop if I were you, Mr. Reynolds," Benzinger said smoothly, hardly raising his voice above dinner-table-conversation level. "Tom, I think Mr. Reynolds is having trouble retrieving something from his pocket. Would you mind helping him?"

Stepping in front to glare into my face, Jones took his gun and stuck it in my left ear. At first, I didn't see the importance of his position. And then I realized, if I managed to spin around, get my vest turned on, and face his gun, that would merely expose my side to Benzinger. They had thought about this meeting, maybe even rehearsed it.

"Take your left hand, remove everything in your right pocket with two fingers, and drop it on the ground," snarled Jones. "Your hand curls around anything, and it'll be the last thing you ever see."

I was gritting my teeth so hard that my jaw was starting to ache. But I saw no way out and soon the defender was on the ground. We repeated the process for the pepper spray.

"And the phone, too," Benzinger droned calmly. Jones grabbed my phone, threw it on the ground, and crushed it under his foot. Benzinger cleared his throat loudly, and as Jones and I looked over, he rubbed his hand over his chest. Even Jones got the message. He tore my jacket and T-shirt open, ripped the headset from my chest, and threw it to the ground. He smashed it under his foot as well.

During the time it had taken Jones to find and destroy all my defenses, Benzinger hadn't said a word even vaguely incriminating. True, his voice would be found in Diane's messages, but this fact alone proved nothing and wouldn't stop him. I swore under my breath for not considering that Benzinger might come along. It was beginning to look like a fatal mistake and my heart started drumming in my ears even more loudly.

Jones had moved in front of me, perhaps four feet away. Benzinger was now on my right at about 10 feet. Even if Benzinger was a lousy shot, he'd probably at least wound me. But if I flipped on the vest, faced him and lunged sideways at Jones, maybe I could knock Jones down. He looked like a small mountain, but he was relaxed, rocking back and forth on his feet.

Perhaps Jones noticed me stealing the glance because he took a couple of steps backward. He was clearly out of range for me to charge.

"Now, let's get to business," said Benzinger. "Tom, stick your gun in Mr. Reynolds' ear again and if he is not taking off that vest in three seconds, see how far his brains fly."

Benzinger was not going to be distracted by idle chatter, so I didn't even let him get to a count of one. I removed the vest and dropped it to the ground.

"Very good," said Benzinger. "Maybe we will get some cooperation and this can all go easily for you and Dr. Stapleton. And now to that issue. Where is she?"

My eyes scanned the area. Perhaps a jogger would come by and I could make a break for it. I doubted they'd shoot me in front of a witness. But I also doubted they'd let me be standing if anyone appeared in the distance. I'd probably be clutching a broken knee among the rubble by the time anyone got near, so I stopped hoping for a passerby. Figuring this would appear to be long enough to deliberate Benzinger's question, I responded.

"She's inside, just like I told Jones."

"I don't think so," spat Benzinger, as he bared his teeth. "That would be too easy. I'll give you one more chance, then we'll all go in together. Unfortunately, if that's the path you take and she's not in there, you'll tell us what we want to know, but you'll never leave. If you want to see her again, the truth this time."

Benzinger didn't have a vest, meaning he would be vulnerable to anything I could find. But throwing a rock at him when he had a gun seemed pointless. I needed to get out of the crossfire, so I could grab the vest and get it turned on. But a way to get both of them on the same side of me? I didn't have a clue. It had been long enough, so I answered.

"It's the truth. She's inside."

"Very well," Benzinger said sighing as if he had given me every opportunity to be spared and I had rejected his generous offer. "Tom, let's get out of public view so you can reason with Mr. Reynolds as necessary."

But at that moment, Diane appeared at the window in the silo, directly above our heads.

"Jeremy, what's going on out there?" She glared down at Benzinger, apparently alerted to his presence by the few words she'd heard on her phone.

"Get back inside," I yelled.

Nothing I had done before this encounter prepared me for this shock. My heart rate soared as my body dumped the last reserve of adrenaline into my bloodstream. My face burned.

My vision narrowed to where I saw only my two adversaries; even Diane slipped from my world. Then, dizziness came crashing down.

The concrete slab that we had used for our table was nearby, so I reached down to steady myself. I tried to think, but my mind wouldn't focus. The only thoughts that remained involved acts of violent desperation.

Perhaps Jones sensed this. Perhaps he knew it from experience, but in the few moments when my mind was black with rage, he covered the distance between us. He hit me like a linebacker, putting the full force of his shoulder into the small of my back. I hit the ground hard, the air knocked from my lungs. Before I could catch my breath, he had secured my hands behind me with some type of plastic tie. He pulled on them until they drew blood and I winced in pain.

Jones then jerked me onto the block of concrete, laying me on my back. Grinding my teeth, I stared up into the cold November sky. I clenched my fists behind me, my hands feeling warm and sticky with blood. At least the pain in my ribs was clearing my head and I knew how Diane had appeared in the window. She must have retrieved the ladder, placed it against the back wall of the silo, climbed up and through the back opening, and then walked across the beam inside. But I wasn't sure what this surmise gained me.

Benzinger's grinning face appeared in my field of vision. My body tensed and I strained against the restraints. "I'm amazed, Reynolds," he said. "I never thought you'd give her up that easily. Looks like I misjudged you. You're more of a sniveling coward than I ever imagined. Tom, go retrieve Dr. Stapleton, and then we can finish this business. I'd say we could just bury them here, but someone might find them someday. And I enjoy jogging here too much to have the trail closed for even an afternoon."

Benzinger moved away and I rolled to my side, so I could watch him and Jones. Pain shot through my wrists with the effort. I could feel the warmth of my body draining out into the concrete block.

Jones started toward the silo, while I searched every conscious corner of my mind, trying to come up with some strategy I could use to help Diane. I was probably lost, but I had nothing for her either. I cursed the day I saw her name online. My only hope was that she had retreated along the route she had come and was now running down the trail a mile away.

"Wait, Tom," said Benzinger. "There's something not right here. I'll get her. You keep the gun on Reynolds. And this time, no talking. Just shoot him. Understand?"

"Got it," said Jones. He obviously didn't care who he killed, as long as he got paid.

Jones took off his vest and started to hand it to Benzinger. But Benzinger hesitated, looking off in the distance. He scratched his forehead, then looked down at the ground at my vest. He grabbed it and put it on.

"I'm taking your vest with me. I don't want Dr. Stapleton standing too close. Who knows what drug-filled syringe she might have on her? When she comes through, don't fall for anything. Don't do anything she says. Don't get near her. Just keep the gun on Reynolds. I'll be right behind."

With my clothes in tatters, I began to shiver. In my disoriented state, Benzinger's actions seemed important, but I couldn't see why. When the fuse blew in my vest, sometime between 19 and 28 seconds, the vest would cease to work. But so what? He'd change to the second vest and be on his merry, murderous way.

Benzinger powered up the vest. I started counting the seconds in my mind because that's what I had planned to do. I was on automatic pilot; nothing else was working. I closed my eyes, trying to clear my head.

Fifteen seconds left.

What if he was ...?

I had the germ of an idea. There were actually three places Benzinger might be when the fuse burned out. Out here. Inside the silo. And in-between. If the fuse blew when he was still in the wall—well, what happened to him depended on what parts of his body were still in transit. But even severing a hand or a foot might create enough confusion for Diane to escape if she hadn't already. It might even distract them enough for me to get away, although I wasn't sure I could. By now, my whole body was shaking from the cold and waves of searing pain were radiating from my ribs.

But I needed to do whatever I could to increase the chance of success. He would be passing through the wall for only a moment, maybe half a second, because it wasn't thick. But I'd have two shots at stopping him if he was trying to both enter and leave between 19 and 28 seconds. Well, at least I knew what I needed to do.

Ten seconds left until the fuse might fail.

He was moving too fast. He'd be going into the silo well before 19 seconds if I didn't slow him down.

"There's a pit, near the back wall. She may try to hide there," I yelled. The words sounded strange, even to my ears. I'm not sure how someone is supposed to sound when sacrificing someone they love without even being asked, but I was certain that blurting it wasn't the right tone.

Benzinger must have thought the same. He turned from the wall and glared at me. He walked back over and looked down. "Giving up your friend is one thing. Helping me find her is another," he growled.

Five seconds left.

He back-handed me across the mouth. Jones laughed. "You're going to curse the day you were born before I'm through with you," snarled Benzinger.

Benzinger stood over me sneering, then stepped back to the wall of the silo. He stood there for a second. I was not about to say anything now. We had passed 19 seconds, so he needed to step through. But he didn't. He just stood there, first looking at the wall, then turning back to glare at me.

Why wasn't he entering? What was wrong? I fought my panic, forcing my mind to the next task—a second countdown. Sometime within the next nine seconds, before he reached 28 seconds of continuous use, the fuse would burn out. He had to enter the building by then or he would be standing outside when the power went off. My mind kept screaming, any time now, any time, as I ticked off the seconds.

Benzinger turned from the wall and came back to stand over me again. "She's waiting there on the other side, isn't she? It's an ambush of some sort."

Concentration was nearly impossible, as my shivering had become uncontrollable, and the pain was assaulting my mind. I closed my eyes, searching for an answer. If I said yes, he'd delay, trying to work out a strategy ... or just wait her out. If I said no, he'd never believe me. Finally, I said nothing. Time was nearly up. By my estimate, he had to enter within the next five seconds. The fuse couldn't last any longer than that.

An evil grin came to his face, as Benzinger made a decision. "Let's see what she does when I come at her from this direction."

And with that, he turned, went to the door on the right—the door in front of the rubble-filled chamber—and stepped through. I stared, almost not believing what I had just seen. Immediately, there was an explosion that filled the air with dust and brought grit raining down on the ground from the silo. In moments, a putrid stench reached my nose.

Some of Benzinger's atoms and those of the vest had merged violently with the construction waste. Other combinations were probably silent, but in the end, it would make no difference. Nothing from the original vests or from the body of Dr. Nils Benzinger would remain as it had been, except for small bits of flesh, bone, or electronics that might be found in the tiny voids within the rubble.

"What happened?" Diane yelled from the opening above us. She was covered in dust and held one hand over her chest, eyes wide in shock. With the other hand, she was clinging tightly to the rope, perhaps wondering if the silo was about to fall.

I spun my head so fast at the sound of her voice that I cut my cheek on the concrete. I hardly noticed the pain. My mind was in such a confused state of exhaustion, feeling overjoyed to see her alive with Benzinger gone and being panicked because Jones was still alive that nothing but confusion remained. I spun to look Jones in the eye, fighting against my restraints. It was no good. They were too tight, I was too weak. My lungs felt ready to explode in my chest as I gasped for air and continued my struggles.

Jones came close. He pulled a knife out of his pocket and opened the blade. It gleamed even in the dim rays of the sun.

Diane screamed.

I yelled, "Run" to her, but my mouth was dry. Hardly a sound escaped my lips. I looked in horror as she slid down the rope, landing 25 feet from the concrete altar where Jones was about to take my life. She started running toward him.

Jones rolled me to my side, pinning one arm to the concrete slab with a vise-like grip. He brought the knife down, slicing the tie from my wrists.

I felt like I should crawl away from him, bring my hands up to defend myself, something, but I couldn't. I rolled onto my back, shaking violently from the cold. My hands were free but still behind me, laying in a warm pool of my own blood.

Diane appeared in front of my face. She was crying. She grabbed the remnants of my jacket by the collar and pulled me closed to her. Her warmth felt like the rays of the summer sun. I tasted the salt of her tears, as they ran down her cheeks and dripped onto my lips.

It's OK, sugar," I croaked and I swallowed hard. I was still dizzy, but the spin was starting to slow. I closed my eyes and gritted my teeth as I pulled one hand from behind my back. I intended to console Diane, but one look at the bloody appendage and I laid it back down on the concrete. Diane looked at me, eyes moist and red. She picked up my hand, kissed each finger, and held it to her chest.

Beyond Diane, I could see Jones walking away. Even in my confused state, this seemed unbelievable. "Wait," I rasped. He stopped and turned back to look at us. "You know what happened?"

"Yeah," he said slowly. "You weren't the first person we had in the study. The other guy had this habit of sticking his head through the Barrier first, so he could see where he was going before he stepped through. Made sense, I guess. But one day in the middle of testing, the vest failed just as he stuck his face through a sheet of glass ...."

"Enough." I didn't need the gory details. Then, I frowned at Jones, not sure how to ask. "And you're just leaving us?" I thought I must be hallucinating.

"Know anyone willing to pay me to kill you?" His tone was mild, calm. Gone was the sing–song taunts that I had come to expect. When I didn't say anything for a moment, he said, "Thought not. Benzinger was a loner. There's no one taking his place. So, I'm out of here; going home. You'll never see me and I'll never see you. But if you do, I'd suggest you walk on by. It would be your word against mine. But I don't like hassles." He had snarled the last words, just as a reminder of how nasty he could be.

Diane helped me sit up and then wrapped me in her jacket. I protested as well as I could, but she wouldn't take it back. She checked my wounds and decided I had some bruised ribs. The rest seemed relatively minor, even if my hands and most of the front of her jacket were covered in blood. She gathered up the necessities, deciding we could return the next day to get the rest. I put my arm around her shoulder and we started limping down the trail toward home.

20. A November vintage

On the first evening after Benzinger entombed himself in the rubble and Jones disappeared, Diane and I did not fulfill our promise to each other for a wild night of passion. Nor did we for the next five nights while my ribs mended and our cuts and scrapes healed. And while full recovery for bruised ribs is generally about a month, by the seventh night, I felt good enough and we started to make up for lost time. She told me that doctors knew things about the human body that no one else did. I thought it was a joke; she convinced me otherwise.

One evening during the second week, post–Benzinger, curiosity got the best of me.

I was seated in the same comfortable chair I had used the night I had accidentally stumbled into Diane's home. Already, she was making the chair mine, often leaving my drink on the table beside it or patting its seat when she wanted to climb into my lap there. Diane was sitting across from me on the couch, her feet tucked under her. Generally, I'd be beside her, letting gravity take its course, but she was reading. She looked very much at peace with only the toes of her socks and her arms appearing outside the lap blanket that covered her.

"Diane, I've been wondering about something," I said.

She looked up from her book, frowning. "How do you always know when I'm getting to the good part?" Then, her look softened and she said, "What is it, honey?"

I hesitated a moment, wondering if there was a better way to phrase my question. I failed to think of one, so I simply asked, "What was your plan when you came back to the silo and appeared at that upper window?"

"Oh. That day." It wasn't that Diane wouldn't or couldn't talk about it, but she didn't like to. Nor did I. But I couldn't get the question out of my mind.

"I really didn't have one," she said slowly, her brows knitted in thought. "I just wanted us to stay alive as long as possible and hoped that we would find a way out." Then she looked up, a slight smile coming to her lips. "But what I've never been able to figure out is how you got Benzinger to put on our vest and go into the other side."

Now, it was my turn to relive those last few moments, and I found myself rubbing my hands together, a wrinkle forming on my forehead. "I didn't get him to wear it," I said, "or go into the other side. It was a case of him overthinking the situation. He was so certain we were playing him that he walked himself into a trap. All I did was try to get him there at the right time."

She looked thoughtful, nodding. "I'm glad that was enough." She went back to her book.

We haven't talked about that day since, and somehow, I don't expect that we ever will. That week living on the edge was enough for both of us. When we need a little thrill now, we just go on a motorcycle ride. The only trouble is, Diane always wants to drive.

Later that second week, I found myself stumped once again. Diane was in the kitchen, quartering an apple for a snack when I came in and took a seat at the island.

She glanced up at me and said, "What's on your mind?"

"It shows?" I chuckled, wondering how she could always read me like a book.

"That something's bothering you? Yeah, a bit."

In the back of my mind, I knew there was a chance this could end in disaster, at least, for me. I took a breath, laid my hands on the counter in front of me, and jumped in. "I'm not certain how to put this but I'm not sure why you don't hate me."

"Seriously?" Her eyes widen, as she stared at me. But I guess looking at my face answered that question. She put the knife down and looked at me closely. "Why would you ask that?"

I sighed again. Breathing seemed to have become somewhat more challenging. "Well, you had everything going for you when we met." Her slight frown told me I needed to adjust that comment slightly. "OK, you were working toward your vision—a stable, rewarding private practice, a nice home, friends and family. And then, I came along and dragged you into, well let's face it, a nightmare. You have to resent that."

She tilted her head, her glance going to the wall over my shoulder. When her eyes returned to mine, she asked, "Didn't we talk about this, right after the mall at that restaurant?"

"Yeah, we did. At the time, you said you believed it was an accident, me leading Jones to you. And it was. But I'm just not sure, in looking back on everything, how you can be so forgiving."

"I see." Her tone was even, matter-of-fact as if she had never thought about what I had done to her before. After a few moments, she said, "What if I had come to you, said I had a problem that I thought you might be able to help me with, using your background in accounting. Would you have helped me?"

My immediate thought was, you're hot and I'd never pass up that opportunity. But I opted to keep my answer short, figuring she could probably guess my initial motivation anyway. "Yes, of course I would."

"OK," she said. "And then later, suppose we found out that I had accidentally, through no fault of my own, involved you in something potentially deadly? Would you have wanted to work with me to get us out of it?"

"Of course. That's the stand you took at the restaurant, and I'd do the same."

"So then, after its all over and we're safe, are you saying you'd reconsider your position and decide you should be angry with me?"

"Well, decide to ... no ... I mean ...." I stopped rambling a moment, trying to collect my thoughts. Finally, I said, "I might wish you had checked out the situation a bit more before involving me."

"And maybe I had that thought too, but that's hindsight. And hindsight's never a good way to judge what we should think now. Don't you agree?" She picked up the knife, rinsed it at the sink, and put it in the dishwasher.

"Well, yeah," I managed to mumble.

She picked up her plate with the quartered apple, gave me a kiss on the cheek, said "Love you," and went back to her reading in the living room. I just sat there for another five minutes, trying to find any way it made sense that I would have wanted to stand by her but she should hate me. I finally gave up, realizing I should just be happy. And I was.

So, after that night, I never looked back again at what we had been through. Instead, I shifted my focus forward and considered what we might become. The next day, I asked Diane if she wanted to live together. She laughed and said she thought we already were. But it seemed like it needed to be asked and answered, and after she said yes, I settled in even more.

After a month with Diane, it felt like home. She seemed more and more at ease in what was soon to be her private practice. She came home daily, giving me the latest news on her patients and what Doris, her administrative assistant, was doing. As for me, the apathy I had lost while running for my life didn't return. Slowly but surely, I was laying out the direction of my future, producing a warmth and closeness of family that I had all but forgotten.

"You're home early," I called, as Diane walked in the front door. I was in the kitchen, sorting the mail as she joined me.

"Yeah, the last patient canceled for the second time. But at least he called. Last time he didn't and Doris charged him for the office visit, so I guess we're making progress." Her voice had trailed off toward the end of the sentence, as she looked at the grin on my face. "So, why do you look like the cat that swallowed the canary?"

"I understand that in the UK, the expression is 'the cat that got the cream.' Did you know that?" I asked, in a mock–serious tone.

"Quit stalling," she said, taking one of her ineffectual swings at me. "Out with it."

"I went over and checked out Dr. Jandrahar's books. He's the vet on Fifth Street?" Diane nodded. "Anyway, the last company that did his accounting was running some really old software. I'll upgrade it and I'm confident I can do his books and yours during the school year and still keep up with classes. Worst case, I farm out some stuff around tax time. I still know a few hungry accountants. And with both jobs, I'd be making about three times what I could at any job on campus."

Diane put her arms around my neck and standing on her tiptoes, she whispered in my ear, "I'm so proud of you." My grin got a bit wider.

"I hoped you would feel that way," I said, as she dropped back to her feet. "I got a nice bottle of wine to celebrate." And I pulled a bottle of wine with a screw cap from beneath the island.

"Oh, yuck," she said, as she turned up her nose. "You bought that wine that we had in the motel? Nostalgia's fine, but not at the cost of the lining of our stomachs."

"Sorry, I couldn't resist your reaction. That stuff was pretty bad, wasn't it?" I pulled an empty of a decent Cabernet from its hiding spot. "I dumped the original and refilled the bottle with this."

"Are you sure the first contents didn't taint the glass?"

"Since the vintage was last month, I don't think there was time for that to happen." Diane laughed, putting her arms around my neck and kissing me lightly.

I grabbed two glasses, poured us each a drink, and we retired to the couch in the living room.

"Before we toast your new job, I have an early Christmas present for you. Have I mentioned that Christmas is less than a week away?" she asked, cocking an eyebrow.

"Five days, 3 hours, 27 minutes, and 11 seconds, I believe you said this morning," I replied. Diane pretended that she didn't hear.

"You worked hard with the registrar to get your pre-vet program down to just a year and a half, counting your previous credits. And I'm not trying to add to your academic load or anything, but I got you another class as a present."

"Another class?" I asked as she handed me a slip of paper. "A class in Tai Chi? That's the meditation-in-motion martial art?"

"Ah, you know," she said grinning at me. "Great for balance and coordination. It might just cut down on your doctor visits ... not that I'm complaining. But I have to warn you. The instructor, she's hard-nosed and doesn't take crap from any student, but I think you'll love her."

"You teach Tai Chi?" I asked.

"I said 'hard-nosed' and you thought of me?" she said, pouting.

"No, you said I'd love her, and I thought of you." I grinned.

By this time in our shared lives, the "L" word had slipped into our vocabulary on a regular basis. Technically speaking, I had been the first to say 'I love you' after we fell through

Diane's bedroom floor in our flight from Jones. But I knew I could argue in front of a jury of my peers that in that context, it hadn't meant much. It was just, 'I love you for such quick thinking.' It hardly meant more than 'I love fried chicken.'

But then, I didn't want to argue in front of a jury or anyone else that my words had meant nothing, because they did. Even then, I had felt a strong attachment to Diane, and it was growing every day. Sometimes I thought about our failed experiment to merge our thoughts and feelings using the vest, and I had a hard time feeling disappointed. Sure, I understood and shared Diane's curiosity about a possible glimpse into another person's psyche. It was an incredible, yet chilling thought. But I knew that I really didn't want to trade the instant intimacy it might provide for the next 50 years of getting to know Diane. Intimacy, to me, is not so much about the destination, as the journey.

"When is the class?" I asked. "I haven't seen you going anywhere."

"It's Wednesday nights. I've been kind of busy lately if you hadn't noticed. I had to get a sub. But I'm back ... make that, we're back to class in two weeks. You know, a year and a half for pre-vet, then four to the degree. You'll be practicing veterinary medicine before you know it."

"I hope it doesn't go too fast."

We placed our glasses on a side table. She tucked her feet under her, and laid her head on my shoulder, her hand caressing my chest. I encircled her with my arms, feeling lost in her warmth, her feel, her smell. This, I knew, was exactly why I didn't want the time to go too fast. I'm not sure exactly why it came to mind, but I asked, "You think we'll see someone else develop something like the vest in our lifetime?"

"I wouldn't be surprised," she said, softly. "If everything was in place for Benzinger, could other labs be far behind?"

"Probably not. I just hope that whoever's next isn't also insane. The potential gains from harnessing that technology are almost unimaginable. I mean, who knows what we might find in the space of an atom."

Acknowledgments

Although perhaps unusual, I'd like to start by recognizing the contribution of an organization, the National Novel Writing Month, or as it's known, NaNoWriMo. And while I didn't really need the encouragement and motivational events they host, as I generally have a hard time getting away from the keyboard during a first draft, it was fun being part of this national event in 2016.

But first drafts are just that and a number of talented individuals had a hand in improving this one. First, I'd like to thank Ms. Janet Harrison and Ms. Helen Shorrocks for reading and providing numerous helpful suggestions. My thanks also go out to Dr. Liz Gehr, who has consistently been there to help me mind my technical Ps and Qs.

Ms. Emma Jaye provided her considerable content editing expertise to help bring the characters and settings alive. If they didn't for you, it's because I didn't listen to her hard enough.

And finally, thanks go to my talented daughter, Ms. Courtney Perrin, for the design and creation of the cover art.

About the Author

Bruce Perrin has been writing for more than twenty-five years, although you will find most of that work only in professional technical journals or conference proceedings. After receiving a Ph.D. in Industrial/Organizational Psychology and completing a career in psychological research and development at a major aerospace company, he's now applying his background to writing novels. Not surprisingly, most of his work falls in the techno-thriller, mystery, and hard science fiction genres, examining the intersection of technology and the human mind now and in the future. Besides writing, Bruce likes to tinker with home automation and is an avid hiker, logging nearly 2,500 miles a year in the first six years of Fitbit ownership. When he is not on the trails, he lives with his wife in St. Louis, MO.

Thank you for reading *In the Space of an Atom*. If you'd like to help others find this story, please consider leaving a review on Amazon, Goodreads, or the website of your favorite bookseller.

For all the latest on my new releases and book reviews, subscribe to my blog: BruceMPerrin.blogspot.com

www.ingramcontent.com/pod-product-compliance
Lightning Source LLC
Chambersburg PA
CBHW071921130726

47909CB00014B/2351